BABY
& other stories
by Paula Bomer

Word Riot Press
Middletown, New Jersey

For Dr. Steven Friedman
and for my father, John Meeks Bomer, (1939-2010)

Baby & Other Stories by Paula Bomer
A Word Riot Press Book
Copyright 2010
ISBN: 978-0-9779343-7-9
LCCN: 2010931732

Word Riot is a monthly online literary magazine dedicated
to the forceful voices of up-and-coming writers. Word Riot
Press is the print extension of the magazine, publishing
chapbooks and paperbacks. For more information please
contact us:

Word Riot/Word Riot Press
PO Box 414
Middletown, NJ 07748
www.wordriot.org
www.wordriot.org/press/

Cover and book design by Ryan W. Bradley
Book was typeset in Walbaum and Garamond
Printed in the U.S.A.

The following stories first appeared in the following journals: "The Mother of His Children" in *Open City*; "She Was Everything to Him" in *Fiction*; "If There Were Two Boats" in *nth position*; "Baby" in *Sub-Lit*; "A Walk to the Cemetery" in *The First City Review*; "Superstition" in *juked*; "The Second Son" in *Pank*; "A Galloping Infection" in *Word Riot*.

CONTENTS

"Count all the factories. An enormous proportion of them produce useless ornaments, carriages, furniture, and trinkets, for women. Millions of people, generations of slaves, perish at hard labor in factories merely to satisfy woman's caprice. Women, like queens, keep nine-tenths of mankind in bondage..."
    --*The Kreutzer Sonata* by Leo Tolstoy

"Woman is the nigger of the world."
    --Yoko Ono

THE MOTHER OF HIS CHILDREN

The car arrived and his wife held the baby on her hip and waved to him as he trotted down their steps. "Call me," she said, and he felt he could smell her coffee mouth and sour breast milk smell as he slipped into the car. She looked old and beat-up, a bit of a double chin resting on her neck. One of her breasts was noticeably larger than the other; this had happened after the birth of their new son, Henry, when her milk came in. He waved back at all of them. Their three-year-old, Jake, bounced around on the sidewalk screaming, "Bye-bye Daddy! Bye-bye Daddy!" He would be gone for only two days. No matter; he was thrilled, thrilled to leave them: stinky, loud and demanding, all of them. And he didn't feel guilty about it. He loved his family, how they were always waiting for him to arrive in the evening. They needed him. He had framed photographs of them on his desk at work. But they were not always that pleasant to be around.

Ted Stanton was the technology director of a Website, thirty-five, balding, and with a limp tire of fat around his middle. He played basketball on Sundays in Brooklyn, near his newly purchased house, with other men in their prime who worked in the online world. They played extremely aggressively, turning red and oozing noxious, booze-scented sweat. They never talked business, but every push, grunt and jump was about whose

IPO was fatter than the others. If he wasn't playing ball on Sundays, he sat. He sat on the subway to and from work, he sat at his desk in his office in a sleek loft in downtown Manhattan, and he sat on the couch at home drinking a beer. He sat at the dinner table where Laura served him dinner almost every night. He then sat in front of the TV, and then sat up in bed and leafed through a magazine. Soon he would be fat. He was convinced Laura wanted him to be fat, as she always presented him with a pint of ice cream and a spoon while they watched TV at night. He hated her for this, but he also was relieved that she was there to take the blame, as he would never want to be responsible himself for getting fat.

He had met Laura five years ago at a party. They discovered that they both lived in studio apartments on Mulberry Street. She was not at all remarkable looking, but her clothes were tight, and her trampy style was unique in his circle of Ivy Leaguers. They slept together that night, at her place. The next morning, deeply hungover, he had to look at a piece of mail on her kitchen counter to get her name. He had forgotten it, or never bothered to ask for it in the first place. They continued to drink a lot and sleep together, and when she accidentally got pregnant, they agreed to go to City Hall and get married. Two years earlier, he would have made her get an abortion. But Ted liked her, liked that she was his, and she cooked him dinner all the time. They had fit well together in bed, and while he knew she was no rocket scientist, he found her simplicity comforting. He had been thirty and eager to marry. He never had much confidence with women, and Laura had made him feel slightly good about himself.

She was just fine in every respect, really. Did he love her? This was a subject matter both Ted and Laura found embarrassing. It was something they had in common, this squeamishness about love. Once, after a particularly gymnastic and satisfying lovemaking session, he had blurted out, "I love you". She answered him, her face muffled into the pillow, something that sounded like "ditto". This was good enough for him, but thereafter he restrained himself from saying anything in the heat of passion.

And now? Now, he was on his way to San Francisco, to a conference. He flew coach and could barely fit into his designated seat. But the flight left on time and no fat people sat next to him—indeed, no one sat next to him. He had a window seat. A pile of magazines and his laptop occupied the seat next to him. His flight attendant was female and despite the globs of make-up on her face, was relatively attractive and not too miserable-seeming. He briefly imagined shoving his dick down her throat. Her tight, navy polyester skirt would rustle loudly as she pulled it up so she could get down on her knees; her shiny, lip-glossed mouth would part as she bent her head back to make room for his erection. It was something he did, imagined violating strange women whom he came into contact with. Once he had even fantasized fucking Larry Worth, the president of his company, in the ass. Larry, chubby, nasty-tempered Larry. Gasping from his smoking habit, the stink of old sweat coming off his dirty boxers as Ted ripped them down and shoved him over his very own desk. The tightness of his asshole, the little pieces of shit clinging to the dark threads of hair. He'd let out one angry scream as Ted stuck him like the pig he was. Larry had been a classmate at Harvard and Ted liked him, but resented him for making more money than himself. He didn't have kids to support. He didn't even have a wife! And definitely not a wife who perhaps defined herself entirely by what she bought.

Besides shopping and minding the children and house, Laura did nothing. In fact, minding the children and house had become a sort of shopping in and of itself. There was new underwear for Jake one day, diapers for the baby the next, and pork chops the day after. Ted knew that taking care of the children and the home was work, regardless of the weekly visits from a Caribbean housekeeper and a part-time babysitter. He wouldn't want to do what Laura was doing. It was thankless, and not only because he didn't really appreciate what she did—which was, in fact, true—but because no one did, not their little children, not the other depressed, defensive, and overeducated mothers she hung out with, not anyone. He was, of course, secretly glad she didn't have a career. But when the sitter came in the morning, Laura went out shopping. And usually, in the afternoon, she strapped the kids in the stroller and shopped some more. She bought nice stuff—Kate Spade diaper bags, Petite Bateau pajamas for the kids, a pair of Gap leather pants for herself. She bought shell steaks, fresh rosemary, organic baby food. She cooked nice dinners with the nice food she bought. But sometimes Ted wondered if there was anyone lurking beneath all that shopping. This kind of thinking made him anxious, and he tried not to go there. He didn't like hyper-intelligent women, but he also liked to think that Laura had a soul.

San Francisco, now there was a nice thought. Ted undid his seatbelt, breathed deeply. Out the airplane window was nothing, a whitish-gray, cloudy nothing. Larry was meeting him at what was promised to Ted to be a very happening restaurant. Larry would bring a crowd of fabulously important shmoozers. There would be lots of parties to go to after dinner, lots of drunk, younger women with interesting jobs. But for some reason, despite the fact that Ted was doing quite well, all those loose party girls, all that fresh lemon pussy, the squeaky young recent college grads with their sixty-grand-a-year jobs, never came on to him. It wasn't because he was married. Plenty of his married colleagues had flings. In the past, his insecurity had made him invisible to women, that he knew. But now he felt as if it were something else. He felt it was because he actually programmed Websites, was a tech guy. All the young women wanted to fuck the creatives, as they were known. It was as if the nature of his job forced him into a monogamous lifestyle he no longer could bear. No one wanted to talk to him about code. Code was not sexy. He didn't want to talk about code either, frankly. It was just something he had a gift for, something he did for a living. And no women, young or old, did technical work. They all worked in marketing or production.

Did he want to divorce Laura? Hmm. Every day he left for work and she stayed home, he felt them grow apart. They grew eight hours apart every day. He, with adults and computers, participating in the world. She, primarily with young children, sinking into a dull, repetitive existence. Besides shopping, she spent a lot of time picking up. She picked up underwear, dirty dishes, toys, old newspapers. She put away the bath towels, lined up the spices in the spice rack, picked the old, bad food out of the refrigerator. Every night she sat cross-legged in front of the refrigerator, perusing its contents.

Once, they had sex in common. That, and socializing. Sex, in many ways, was what had brought Laura and him together. Sure, they were both white, educated and upper-middle class. They both believed in the superiority of all things New York. But it was their fucking that really clinched the deal, the negotiation which was their marriage.

"Something to drink?"

It was early. He knew the flight attendant really meant juice or coffee, but he ordered a Bloody Mary. There she was, with her full cart, leaning over to find a miniature bottle of vodka. She smiled at him. He wanted her to care that he was ordering a drink so early; he wanted her to feel his pain, see him as slightly on the edge. But what did she care if he had a drink first thing in the morning? He was nothing to her. She placed the little plastic cup with the rounded ice cubes onto a napkin, leaning again to do so, this time over his pile of stuff on the seat next to him. She had nice tits. She smiled, revealing a slight overbite. Perhaps the overbite was why he had imagined putting his dick in her mouth. The extra room there, the sexiness of the imperfection. Perhaps she secretly hated men who drank, he thought. Perhaps her father was a drunk who beat her, molested her. He wanted her to care.

The drink tasted good. Slightly horseradish-y, very cold. The plastic cup was like a feather in his hand. He felt wild, free. He pushed the little silver button on the armrest and leaned back. Someone behind him coughed in annoyance and Ted looked behind him. Some guy with a job, like himself. Angry in his little seat, jowly face in his newspaper. Fuck him, Ted thought, and pushed the seat back further, as far as it would go. The back of his seat at this point, he knew, was in the guy's lap. Ted coughed back at him.

An ice cube from his drink fell in his lap. Ted felt it there, felt it cold and hard, making a dark stain on his trousers. He picked it up off of his pants and put it back in his cup. Then he downed his drink.

When they had decided to keep the baby, Laura had been thrilled. She glowed in those first few months, despite her upset stomach, she positively glowed. She quit drinking, smoking and cut back on her coffee intake. She started watching lots of TV. As she grew larger, they both grew more anxious. Ted worked late at night. Laura began looking for a house in Brooklyn, as the tiny apartment in Manhattan would no longer suffice. She took a prenatal yoga class where she met other expectant moms. She bought baby clothes, researched strollers and car seats. Her life, which once was partying and flirting, turned into obsessive nesting activities. Ted continued to work late and became ambitious in a way he'd never been before. He asked for a huge raise and got it. He wanted a corner office. He, too, became obsessed, obsessed with making more money.

And sex? They continued to have sex, albeit more cautiously, less frequently and toward the end of her pregnancy, not at all. The last time they had sex during the pregnancy had been late at night, under the covers. Laura's back was facing him as they lay side by side. It took about two seconds before he came. Her pussy had felt so swollen, and so thick with mucous, that it freaked him out. It had felt good, in a way, but alarmingly different and almost completely animal, or something. Like he was fucking a sheep. Overall, it was an unpleasant interaction, regardless of the physical gratification.

As Laura's due date neared, they began attending a birth class. Laura had researched various birth classes—this was one of those things she talked at him about, which class to take, which hospital to have the baby in, to get an epidural or no epidural. Ted did not understand all the hoopla about birth. It was after the birth that things really started to happen, wasn't it? After the baby arrived, that's what really mattered. When he spoke this way to her, Laura would get mad, saying, "It's not your body, so you just don't care. You don't care about me, do you? You don't know how to care about me!" Then she would storm into the living room and turn on the TV. End of discussion.

The birth class met once a week in an elementary public school in the West Village. Ted hated it. The "instructor", Jane, was a beady-eyed, colorless woman in her forties who was relentlessly cheerful about birth despite an incredibly strong hostility that emanated from her person. Sometimes, one of her children attended the class and would sit in a loft in the back of the room playing by himself while his mother talked excitedly about vaginas, the uterus, dilation, effacement, placenta, and the like. Ted was disgusted. All the other couples seemed pleased as punch. Then came the practice sessions. Laura would lie on her side and he sat next to her, rubbing her back and talking to her in a soothing voice about oceans and forests. He just didn't get it. Couldn't she just take some drugs and put a sheet over her?

The flight attendant loomed over him suddenly. He ordered another Bloody Mary. She didn't make eye contact with him this time. Good. Maybe she did care, he thought, pouring the vodka into the tomato juice and stirring. His hand shook slightly as he banged the little plastic stirrer around. Bloody Mary. Bloody bloody. At the end of the birth class, they'd watched videos of births. Ted would close his eyes. Instructor Jane, and sometimes some of the other women, cried and exclaimed, "Isn't it beautiful?" Ted ran off to the bathroom, thinking he might throw up.

He tried to talk to Laura about it. It's not that he didn't want children, he just didn't want to watch them come out of her. Was that so wrong? He admitted, bravely he thought, that he was scared. Laura argued that he would be sad and feel left out if he wasn't there watching.

"What if you don't bond with our son because you're too chicken to see him come into the world?" She'd been sniffly and angry, with only weeks to go before the birth.

"I can't wait to meet this baby," He'd said. "I'm not worried about loving this baby or not. I just am nervous about the whole birth thing. You are too, admit it. You're not so sure it's going to be so beautiful."

"I don't want to be alone, Ted. And I think the immediate bonding thing is real. I want you there in the room with me, helping to deliver this child."

"Instructor Jane is brainwashing you! My dad loved us! He wasn't in the room watching us slither out of my mother's crotch!" He hadn't meant to yell. Laura burst into tears. That was it. He apologized and said he'd do his best. And he did. At the hospital, he held her hand, gave her ice chips, and told her stories of mountains and trickling rain until she screamed at him to shut the fuck up. Jake's head appeared and his wife, huffing, deranged, and drug-free, touched Jake's head. The midwife told Ted to touch Jake's head, too, and he did. A wet, hairy, little head, stuck in the pelvic bone of his wife. He didn't like it. The room smelled of feces and some weird, thick metallic smell; the smell of fear, the smell of blood and earth. His wife's vagina expanded into something entirely unrecognizable as his son's body emerged. Her vagina was all blood and ooze, as wide as a house, and beet red except for the places where it was a dark, bruised purple; looking at it just made Ted hurt all over. Laura's eyes bulged from her face, black-green veins glistened all over her round stomach and breasts. Dark streaks of shit, poorly wiped off by the nurse, lay smeared on her buttocks and her once tiny pink rosebud of an asshole was swollen to the size of a small melon. She moaned as if she were dying. He began to fear that she was dying. He had weird thoughts wishing that she would die, just so the damn thing would be over with, and so that he never had to look her in the face again. The midwife yelled, "Take a picture, take a picture!" He had been given a camera by his wife. He didn't want to take a picture. He wanted to curl up in a ball and disappear. Everybody was screaming. Laura was no longer Laura. Her voice came from a place he'd never known was in her. He couldn't stand it. He couldn't stand looking at anyone anymore, and he began backing out of the room, the bitter taste of vomit on the back of his throat. His wife began screaming, "I'm dying! I'm dying! Pull! Pull him out of me!" Minutes later, he held his newborn son. The midwife asked him to take off his shirt first, for some "skin on skin contact". He ignored her. Jake, their little boy, their perfect tiny boy, squeaked and cried. Holding him was, undoubtedly, the most profound experience of his life. Nothing could touch that. But the birth itself rattled him. He had been afraid and now he was, well, traumatized.

The constant whir of the airplane reminded Ted of the computers at work. A soothing, white noise. He was fifteen the first time he touched pussy. A Saturday night, in the graveyard behind Hotchkiss. His first year of boarding school. She was a lovely, bulimic, Greenwich, Connecticut girl named Mary Todd. They had been drinking vodka mixed with 7Up. After fumbling around for awhile, Ted, so nervously, put a finger into her panties, searching for it. It was warmer than he

thought it would be. No one had told him it would
be warm in there. Slippery yes, but with invisible,
super-fine grains of sand. He let his finger linger
there as Mary Todd sighed underneath him. His
erection waned as his hand explored, but his
curiosity was sated. Like a blind man, he saw with
his fingers.

In the year that followed Jake's birth, they
went to a marriage counselor, a sex therapist, and
finally, a doe-eyed, extremely short woman in
Times Square who specialized in post-birth male
sexual trauma. She reminded Ted of Dr. Ruth and
he often had to stop himself from breaking into
nervous laughter during their sessions with her.
He did this by thinking about death. Death, Ted
would think, frowning in concentration. We all
will die, we all will die, was his mantra. Laura
and he spent a lot of time there watching explicit,
touchy-feely sexual technique videos while the
therapist pointed to a close-up of a penis thrusting
in and out of a vagina and said stuff like, "See? It's
not a bad thing, the vagina. It's friendly!" Indeed,
the vagina had once been his friend. And to a
certain extent, the vagina became his friend
again. Only on occasion now did he become
erectally challenged, so to speak. Only on
occasion was he haunted with the specter of
Jake's birth. Henry, the new baby, was born while
he waited outside. His wife had an epidural and
read magazines throughout the labor. The Dr.
Ruth look-alike had convinced Laura that Ted
needed some boundaries, and that this did not

mean he was a bad husband, nor did it mean he was an unloving father. Ted was so thankful for this, so thankful for the support he didn't even know he needed, so thankful that someone had articulated what he felt, that she became a powerful goddess in his dreams. He dreamt of her often, even though he couldn't remember her name. In his dreams, she stroked his head and her voice was the soothing voice of his mother.

The white-gray nothing outside of the tiny window was changing. Bits of land and water became discernible. Ted looked down at his drink. It was gone. At some point, the flight attendant had put a little box with a sandwich, an apple and a cookie on the tray next to him. Where had he been? He rubbed his eyes. Had he slept? San Francisco was approaching. Suddenly, he felt drunk and sad. He missed Jake, he missed the drooly, gurgly new Henry. And in a lesser way, he missed his bossy, aging, somewhat boring wife. She was, after all, the mother of his children. She was a decent, hard-working mother. He picked up the sandwich and started to eat it. He would catch up on sleep in his eco-sensitive hotel. He would drink maybe a little too much at the parties, but not enough to behave inappropriately. He would not get laid, this he knew for certain, because he truly wasn't interested in acquainting himself with the vagina of some strange person. And when he returned home, what to do with Laura's straightforward longings directed toward him? Her foot on his crotch at night? Her rubbery, milky, lopsided breasts pushed against his back as they lay in bed? Said or unsaid, he had grown to love this woman. He did not always like her, this was true. He had stared deep into her, watched her produce life and it had changed him. He knew, like never before, that he would die, Laura too would die, and that even his children were temporary beasts of the earth themselves. His job, their house, basketball, preschool and shopping— it was all just waiting, killing time. And while he waited? He would do his best. That's all he could do.

The flight attendant came by to pick up his empty cup. Ted, after wiping up the little drips of boozy tomato juice from the tray, neatly stuck the napkin and the tiny vodka bottle into the empty cup. He was trying to be helpful. He lifted his arms to her with his garbage, to save her the trouble of reaching over for everything.

"Thank you." he said, his eyes wet with vodka, and the plane continued to descend.

THE SHITTY HANDSHAKE

She saw Peter rise from the depths of the subway station, a dark, pasty figure into the bright, finally warm, spring day. It was Brooklyn in early May, a lovely Tuesday, and he saw her at the same moment she saw him. Rarely had she seen him in daylight, if ever. He wore a tattered gray shirt and loose jeans; a reddish blond stubble covered his face. Karen was pushing a stroller with her big baby in it, and her three-year old clung to the metal bar of the pram, squinting in the bright light.

He waved half-heartedly. She waved back. She was past him now. And then she swung her stroller around, a fine sweat forming under her arms, and lurched toward him.

"Peter", she said.

"Hey." He looked like utter shit. It was eleven in the morning, and he was just getting back from work.

He worked nights, this she knew. He worked at a printing press in Tribeca. They had been friendly pool buddies at the bar near her house. They played against each other often—he won most of the time, but when Karen beat him, which she did more than just occasionally, it had always felt very sexy.

She leaned into him, into his face. He pulled back a bit, out of surprise, but not with much force. With her mouth next to his ear, she could smell a stale unpleasant scent coming off of his hair. She closed her eyes and for a moment, the sun and new spring day vanished and she was back at the bar, smoking cigarette after cigarette, shooting pool, drinking vodka and cranberries in a pint glass late into the night.

"I want to fuck you." she said, quietly, and then she grabbed his neck and quickly bit his ear.

"When?"

"I'll call you." And with that, she turned back around, and made her way down Smith Street to Carroll Park.

Karen Valence had married a man who didn't love her. Perhaps worse, she had married a man who had a shitty handshake. Come to think of it, the boyfriend she almost married before she married Dan had a shitty handshake as well. The thing that she had always thought of as the indicator of character, of manliness, was the handshake. Both Dan and Sam (the man before Dan) had these limp-wristed, warm, damp handshakes. And they never put out their hands first. No, they waited until someone else, some hardy man or confident woman, thrust a hand at them. And then—well, Karen could see the disappointment on the other person's face. And she sympathized. She hated shitty handshakes. She was from the Midwest! People from the Midwest didn't have shitty handshakes, unless they were a drug dealer, a particular type of snively housewife, or gay.

Maybe they were gay, her husband, her ex-boyfriend. Maybe that was why she was unhappy.

Peter had a real handshake. Looked you straight in the eye, a firm grip. He was from Ohio, dammit. He was a real man. Funny, how she hated the Midwest when she lived there and now she was so nostalgic for it. In fact, most everyone she was drawn to in New York was from the Midwest. Which was different than living there. Perhaps everyone worthwhile knew to leave, but then brought something special with them. A good handshake, for one.

She'd quit drinking in February. She quit because she was tired of looking at her children in the morning, hungover and fearing sudden heart failure or, at the very least, of vomiting up her breakfast. She called up Tom Frohm, a writer like herself, whom she knew was in AA. He agreed to take her to her first meeting. Dan had stayed home from work so she could go to a meeting. The night before, she'd told Dan that she was going out to get some milk. She'd gone to the grocery on the corner and bought milk and then walked straight to the bar and drank vodka and cranberry until four in the morning. It had been a good night, what she remembered of it. But she didn't remember much. And the hazy parts scared her. Dan had fallen asleep on the couch, in the living room. He said he was worried.

When she thought about Dan worrying about her, she knew why. Who would take care of the kids? Who would buy him underwear, who would feed him? These were the things he worried about.

The AA meeting was a "speaker" meeting, Tom explained, where one person told his or her story in detail and afterward, everyone could share in relation to his experiences. Karen looked up to Tom. He'd published two novels. She'd only published two short stories. They sat on folding chairs in a chapel in Brooklyn Heights. Karen's hangover made everything seem sacred; the coolness of the room, the sloppy circle the chairs made. Her vision was still blurry, her heart beats erratic. She often got weepy and religious during hangovers. Life seemed so delicate! So fragile and tender, like a baby lamb about to be slaughtered! And yet, she could pour a bottle of vodka into herself and still not die.

"A speaker meeting. OK." She smiled at him.

He didn't smile back. In fact, he seemed to recoil from her as if she had some disease. Later, he and everyone else would explain they thought she did have a disease, and so did they. Meanwhile, he looked at her with disgust and loathing. "You just listen. In the beginning, you need to do a lot of listening."

Karen nodded sheepishly. Why was he looking at her like she was the devil?

"I've been sober for ten years, but we are all only one drink away from our next drunk." he said unconvincingly, holding his chin very high.

She was ashamed, nauseous, and terrified. And yet, at the beginning of the meeting, before the speaker took over and everyone was introducing themselves, she raised her hand and gratefully declared, "My name is Karen, and I'm an alcoholic." It felt wonderful! She had always drunk a lot, from a very early age. She had always loved drinking and had problems ending a session of drinking. Yes, she thought! I'm an alcoholic! Yes!

Things went downhill from there. She attended meetings every day, as she was told to. But as the meetings piled up, so did a creeping feeling that everyone in them was full of horseshit. Not more full of horseshit than any other group of people, but still. She was a writer for a reason—she loathed groups of people. But she gave it a try and there were things she liked. She liked sitting around, talking about drinking excesses. She liked the vile honesty of it. But what felt disingenuous was the across-the-board regret. It seemed forced. Didn't any of these people ever *like* drinking? So much of the talk seemed like wistful nostalgia carefully clothed in shame and repentance. Despite her misgivings, she liked the prayers. She loved the prayers. Praying alone curled up on her side of the bed at night wasn't the same. Praying with others, holding hands—it made tears well up in her eyes, it felt so good.

A few weeks into it, uncharacteristically, Tom called her. "How's it going?"

"Well, I'm not feeling so connected to the whole AA thing."

There was a pause.

Karen continued, "But I haven't started to drink again, if that's what you mean."

"Good, good. The important thing is to go to the meetings and not drink. That's what it's all about."

Occasionally, she went to a meeting where some truly hardcore lush went on to explain how much better his life was now that he wasn't completely shitfaced day and night and in and out of jail. Now that he wasn't playing with firearms and beating up his family members. These meetings made sense to her. But others didn't.

Like the beginners meetings that she was told to go to.

She had been told she needed to go to one because, once, she raised her hand during an "open" meeting and talked about how she had been thinking of drinking again. This was not good. People came up to her after the meeting, their faces stern and reprimanding. "You need to go to a beginners meeting," one after another said. She seemed confused. Wasn't AA supposed to be about talking about one's problems with alcohol?

Later that day she called Tom and relayed her confusion.

"It seemed as if people were upset that I mentioned drinking. Or that I wanted to drink."

"Well, AA isn't for everybody. In fact, in the Big Book, they talk about how some people are just not capable of being honest with themselves. Maybe you are one of those people," he said, bitterly. "Listen, I have to go. And please don't call me anymore. In AA, you are really only supposed to talk to other women about your problems. It's in the literature, which you should read. Men talk to men. Women talk to women." Then he hung up.

Well, Tom hated her, this she had always known. He thought her an obsequious loser, a pathetic no-talent. Just because he used to have a drinking problem and she had one now didn't change that matter.

And Karen was frightened of other women as a general rule. She had female friends, but not vast networks of them. She just wasn't a girl's girl. She had never gone to the bathroom in groups. She had never mastered the art of gossip. She liked men. Straight men. She liked men who wanted to fuck her the most.

Meanwhile, at home, things didn't seem much better. Sure, she wasn't sick on the occasional morning. But she felt she never had anything to look forward to. She felt...deprived. This was something she tried to talk about at meetings, including the beginners' meetings she traveled to Park Slope to attend.

In the mornings, she tried to say a prayer. Thank you God, for helping me not be hungover.

She did like waking up, feeling healthy. But then she'd look in the mirror as she splashed cold water on her face and think, I look old. I look fucking old. Her eyes were puffy, her chin looked jowly. Her breasts looked battered after nursing two children and her stomach was lined. She looked like someone who didn't deserve to get laid. But that's what she wanted more than anything—to get righteously fucked.

"Life on life's terms," a twenty-five year old Harvard graduate chirped knowingly at her after a beginners' meeting. She was the leader of the beginners' meeting and she had walked up to Karen when it was over, her arms folded bitchily across her chest. She'd been leading the group for almost a year. "Life on life's terms," she repeated and shook her head in a frustrated manner. This was after Karen had talked about the difficulty of seeing herself so clearly, for who she was in a physical sense. Karen turned red. Every time she tried to talk about her problems, someone was a complete asshole to her.

The Harvard girl had told her story once. It went something like this: she used to smoke pot at night. Almost every night! A few hits from a little one-hitter that she always had with her! She actually hated alcohol. Smoking a bit of grass regularly when you are twenty-five did not seem like something horrible to Karen. In fact, it seemed normal. People who didn't smoke pot in college or their early twenties were the real crazies, thought Karen. In Karen's estimation, what the uptight Ivy Leaguer needed was a good ass-fucking. Not an itty bitty bit of marijuana.

Karen was starting not to believe. She had to bite her tongue at almost every meeting. If she couldn't say anything without getting admonished by smart-assed young women, then she would just not go anymore. It was humiliating—in many ways more humiliating than drinking had been.

She decided not to go to meetings.

She talked to Dan about it. "Whatever you think is best, honey", he said, not looking up from the newspaper. Now that dinner was served, and laundry laundered, Dan had stopped worrying about her. Or anything, for that matter.

Sometimes, she thought that drinking was the only thing that kept her marriage together. Not drinking not only made her notice her aging, but it made her notice how much she loathed Dan. And drinking was such a good way to hate herself, which was a nice break from hating her husband. When she drank, she could feel that the world cared about her, revolved around her and her misdeeds. Sober, the cold reality of the indifference of the universe of people stung. She did believe in God, she always had. But if the benign love of God was supposed to be enough, then why were they all there in a group, holding hands and praying together? No amount of group meetings could cushion the raw coldness she felt. Indeed, they'd seemed to strengthen it.

Paula Bomer

Dan came home from work late. It was nine o'clock on Thursday. It seemed as if it had just gotten dark, that's how long the days felt already. The children were asleep. He liked that, coming home to a quiet house. He worked late often.

"I'm going to a meeting," Karen said.

"I thought you stopped going to those," he said, as he snooped around the kitchen looking for food. "What's for dinner?"

God, how she hated feeding him. He was like a dog, only worse. There was no animal innocence. Dogs at least gratefully wagged their tails.

"I didn't make dinner," Karen said. Her lips were wet with gloss, her legs shaved.

"What?" he said, and he looked up at her, confused. She'd spoiled him, having dinner ready all the time. In some ways, his childish behavior felt like her fault. And then she remembered—he was supposed to be her husband, not her child.

I'm going to die not knowing what it means to be loved. I'm going to die unhappy, afraid and alone. I'm going to die without having published a book. These were the thoughts that went through her head as she walked to Peter's apartment. And yet, she had never felt so alive with possibility. Every step she took felt meaningful. The sounds of the cars in the spring air were as beautiful as any bird's song. Garbage swirled on the cement, gracefully accompanying the music of the city at night—the honking cars, the hollering in Spanish, the rumble of a train underground.

Peter lived in Fort Greene, about a twenty-minute walk from her more gentrified Cobble Hill neighborhood. He let her into his apartment—a spare place littered with canvas and paintings. His paintings were good. Peter smelled like whiskey. He had a tiny glass of it, with lots of ice. From it, he took sips, just wetting his lips.

"Would you like a drink?"

"No thanks."

Later, when they were in bed, he sat up on his haunches. He put a finger inside her, ceremoniously, and then sucked on it. "You. You have a pussy. The real thing, woman."

Then he turned her over on her stomach, raising her hips into the air, and proceeded to give her head.

The next day, her sister-in-law called. She hated her sister-in-law. Her name was Alexis, and she was, more or less, the nastiest person Karen had ever met. You can take a girl out of the Upper East Side (she lived in LA now) but you can't take the Upper East Side out of the girl. For years, she tried to get along with Dan's family members. Years. Yet it seemed every year they were more horrible to her than the year before. When she quit drinking, she decided to quit trying with them. All this wasted energy! And for what? To be mentally bitch-slapped by a bunch of ugly, chinless women who would never like her, no matter what she did to try and please them? In fact, she'd become increasingly aware that trying to please them was the problem. They loathed kindness: they loathed effort. And here she'd been combining the two things together, wrongly thinking it was the way to be a decent human in the world.

"Hello, Karen? It's Alexis," she chimed, her lockjaw so strong that just listening to her immediately made Karen's neck ache.

"Hi Alexis," Karen said.

"How are you?"

Here was where Karen was supposed to say, *I'm well*. But she couldn't. She hated to say, *very well, and you?* In that singsong way, like they were watching Mary Poppins.

"I'm *good*, and *you*?" She said good so that it rhymed with thud.

"Very *well*, thank you."

There was a pause. Karen shut her eyes. God, please let booze miraculously start pouring itself down her throat, like from heaven. Please God. Sometimes the wrong prayers just slipped out of her mind, unbidden. What was she to do?

"We were wondering if you'd like to join us on the Cape for a bit this summer. We'd *loove* to see you. And Adrienne will be there. So the kids will have *lots* of fun."

Lots sounded like *luts*. Adrienne was their much-abused nanny, who often worked Christmas, Thanksgiving, day, night—you name it, she was there. She was always there. Karen actually liked her, but it wasn't enough. Hanging out in the back room with a nice but pitiful nanny did not constitute a vacation. And that's what happened when she spent time with Dan's family. She ended up in the back room with the nanny, after everyone had "seen" the children, and then later, she ended up doing dishes.

"Thanks, Alexis. But I don't think I can make it. You should check with Dan, though. I'm sure he would love to go."

"You have other *plannz*?"

"Actually, no. I just don't think I'd be comfortable, but thanks. You have Dan's work number, yes?"

"I think so." Again, with the pause. What did Alexis want her to say? What was with the pause? Then Alexis continued: "You wouldn't be comfortable?" Karen could hear her sister-in-law adjust her headband.

"No."

"I'm sorry. But why not?" Alexis said this very purposefully. She had been a fierce field hockey player at boarding school. Occasionally, a bit of courage showed itself.

"Because I'm not comfortable around you and your family."

Silence.

"I'm sorry." Alexis said, with absolutely no conviction. Indeed, it was one of those sorrys that really meant fuck you.

"No need to be sorry. I'm just not comfortable around you and there's nothing either of us can do about it."

"Well, *but* why not? We're always so happy to have you," she lied.

"Because you are a bitch and a snob."

"I beg your pardon?"

"I'm not comfortable around you because you're a bitch and a snob. There's nothing anyone can do about that at this point. It's just who you are, what you are. A bitch, and a snob." Karen's ears started to ring. A current of electricity surged through her and the lights in the kitchen flickered. The truth was that powerful. Because you are a fucking stuck-up cunt, she thought. Because you think your shit doesn't smell. Because you are an evil, social climbing, soulless whore of the devil.

When she got off the phone, she was so high she realized she didn't need booze. No, she just needed to tell the truth. It was such a rare thing, the bald truth, especially since she'd gotten older.

Of course, the feeling wore off, just like the effects of alcohol do. It only took two days for the heavy feeling of repression to weigh her down again. She was polite to the nursery school teacher, to the girl at the grocery store. She tried to be patient with her kids, even if inside she was seething with impatience. And so.

She decided to start drinking again. If she was going to get turned over on her stomach and get eaten out by a man who clearly loved what he was doing—and thank you, God, she was going to! She had the real thing, he said so!—than she was going to need some fortification.

The first drink was a beer, while cooking dinner for the kids. It was the best beer she'd ever had in her life. A can of Foster's, a monster of a beer. It tasted as sweet and blessed as heaven. The sun shone in her kitchen, and she turned on some music, piano concertos by Ravel, and she hummed and spooned out noodles to her three-year-old daughter, Sadie, and her nine-month-old son, Nat. Her happiness was infectious—the little things ate well, giggled, didn't cry. Which was a miracle, really. Her children cried often, particularly her son. What else was a nine-month-old going to do? Talk things over reasonably? Of course he cried. But not tonight, no. The beer had changed things.

When Dan came home, he put an arm around her.

"You're drinking?"

"Yes." She was shitfaced. One beer—well, really, one beer the size of two—and she was completely shitfaced.

"You know, my sister called me at the office today. She said she spoke with you last week."

"Really? I need to go downstairs. I just had an idea for a story. I'll be up in a minute."

Karen went downstairs to her office. She turned on the computer. She hadn't written anything in months. In fact, she hadn't written anything since she quit drinking in February. The computer swayed in front of her. It took awhile, but she managed to open a Word document. This encouraged her. She wrote, "I am drunk." Then she lay herself on the small couch next to the desk and fell asleep.

Things progressed rapidly from there. The beer turned into a beer and then some wine. The children, who at first fed off of her newly light and joyous mood, now started to act out to get her attention as she stared blearily at them. Nat threw his spoon down on the floor and looked at her. Sadie hit her brother. If Karen reacted harshly, if she yelled or swatted, she'd drown out the shame with another glass of wine. If she didn't react badly, she rewarded herself with another glass of wine. It all made sense.

Dan came home and she took to going downstairs to her office. This seemed to please Dan, thinking his wife was back to her creative work. Usually, she just got online and read things, but he didn't know that. Occasionally, she used to think, why did I marry him? She tried to remember the events leading up to their marriage. The only things she could come up with were: one, she was young and stupid, and two, she accidentally got knocked up. But there had to be something else, there had to be.

She'd been *flattered*. How could a nice man from a nice family like a girl like her? A girl from Ohio, whose father sold truck parts? Ego had been her downfall. Pride was the reason for the very existence of the devil. Occasionally, she tried to feel sympathy for the young woman she'd been. She tried to understand that she hadn't been entirely stupid even if she married the first man who would have her. She'd been not only flattered, but also afraid. She didn't want to be alone. And now, she was more alone than she could have ever imagined.

But why did Dan marry her? Clearly he had no respect for her, she'd discovered that as the years had gone on. But maybe that had been the point. To marry someone you had so little regard for, that you could still, essentially, be entirely loyal to your mother, to your sister, to your superior clan. To marry someone who posed no threat. To marry someone who will take care of your house, mop your floors, wipe your children's bottoms—a nanny and a maid. And a whore, in the beginning. Yes, she'd been his whore, too.

One night, in her office, she read an article about a house in Pennsylvania that blew up. A grandfather who was a retired minister, and his wife and their three-year-old grandchild all died in the explosion. No one knew why the house blew up; it just did. This made sense to her, things blowing up for no reason. Why didn't it happen more often? She had always thought everything could blow up at any minute. Houses, cars. Ovens, too. It was one of the reasons she didn't get her driver's license until she was thirty. It was one of the reasons why she preferred to cook in their toaster oven.

After a Foster's and some wine one night, the kids were already bathed and read to, but not yet asleep. She heard Dan come in and she ran down the stairs.

"I'm going out." She said.

"Where to?"

She wanted to say, none of your fucking business, but Sadie sat curled up on the stairs, attentively looking at them.

"To a meeting."

"But you've been drinking."

"I know. That's OK," she said, already out the door.

"Would you like a drink?" he asked.

"Yes!" she said.

Peter held both of her breasts in one hand, that's how big his hand was, and that's how tightly he squeezed her. Her whole body tensed. Then he put his other hand firmly on her neck. She gasped, but she could breathe.

She'd never come so hard in her life.

Later, he asked, "How come I never see you at the bar anymore?"

"I stopped going there. I don't know."

Afterward, they sat up in his bed, sipping whiskey after whiskey. The TV was on as they lay in the dark. The Comedy Channel. She could smell the yeasty smell of his naked body, pressed absentmindedly against her own. It was a warm night. Good God, it was summer! Summer again! She had more whiskey. And more.

When she woke, she was on top of the sheets, sweating. Peter lay under the covers, his back turned to her. The light was gray in the apartment; it was barely dawn.

As she walked back to Cobble Hill, her arms wrapped around herself in the cool morning air, she was struck with how her head hurt. Her vision circled and tunneled. She tried to lick her lips but her tongue was dry. She was hungover. The first real hangover since she started drinking again. Her heart began pounding wildly and her torso began shaking. She sat down on someone's stoop on State Street and closed her eyes. She put her head to her arm and smelled the sweet, sticky whiskey sweating out of her pores. She started to force her breath to come in and go out slowly. This helped a bit. Then she closed her eyes, and she comforted herself with an image of her body, clean and smooth on the outside, a husk, with her poisonous insides scraped, gone. With just a pure emptiness inside the shell of her skin. As she stood up to start the walk home, she imagined her empty body filled with the light of the day.

Before Dan left for work, he said, "We need to talk."

He looked scared, but determined. He was an earnest man, who went through the motions of being normal with a ferocity that Karen found outrageous. How can someone behave like nothing is wrong when houses and ovens blow up for no reason? When your life is falling apart, very clearly, before your eyes?

The children were eating cereal. Karen swallowed an aspirin and gagged. She managed not to throw up the little white pill, but her heart began pounding furiously. She went to the couch and sat down.

Sadie came over to her.

"Are you OK, mommy?"

"Yes. I just had a coughing fit. But I'm OK."

Sadie pulled herself up on her mother's lap. Karen's heart started to pound again. She'd never felt anything so heavy in her life, this daughter of hers on her lap.

"You look old, mommy." Sadie said.

"I am old."

"Yes, but today you look like Grandma." Sadie said, looking sad. "Here," she said, tracing her tiny finger next to her mother's mouth. "Right here is where you look like Granny."

After turning on cartoons for the kids, she went down to her office and turned on the computer. She wrote, "I am miserable." Then she started surfing the Web. She read an article, "Top Five Signs Your Spouse is Cheating". One: She becomes more affectionate. Two: She starts wearing her wedding band more often. Three: She starts wearing fancy underwear. And so on. In other words, if Karen were to suddenly act nicely to Dan and start caring about the way she looked, he'd figure out that she was fucking someone else. This perplexed her. Why bother? Why not just get it over with? She looked down at her finger, a thin gold ring around it. She never thought about it, the ring, that is. Hell, she hadn't thought about it for years.

That night, when Dan came home, late like always—the kids were long asleep—she threw her wedding band at him. It hit him in the eye.

"Jesus! What the hell was that about?" He asked. He hadn't quite made it inside yet.

"I'm fucking someone else. So go fuck yourself," she said, and exited her home as he still held onto the door.

Violence toward men was understandable if the men were violent first. Karen remembered seeing *Thelma and Louise* and being disappointed. You have to be nearly raped to make it OK to kill them? But that's how it was.

Karen had been date raped in college once. She'd been drinking a lot and it all was very hazy. She remembered bringing the older brother of a girlfriend of hers back to her room and then she remembered him fucking her, much to her dismay. She didn't fight it in any sort of vicious way, that she could remember, but she didn't want it, either. And that was nothing compared to the daily life of small hells she lived with Dan.

The morning after the rape, she was angry and ashamed. But she didn't want to kill the guy. Dan, on the other hand, inspired crazy, murderous fantasies. It was the gentle stupidity of "nice" men that robbed her of any feelings of mercy. An asshole was an asshole and it was all so straightforward. You stayed away, you had no regrets, no one questioned you. But what about the Dans of the world? What to do with them?

When she thought of divorce, she imagined herself so free! Images of herself flying in a blue sky dotted with clouds, light as a feather, would occupy her thoughts. She imagined herself free of the burden of his things—free of his socks, his briefcase, his belts and shoes. Often, she daydreamed of his being gone, of his being killed accidentally in a subway explosion, or a car accident.

But truthfully, she feared it more than wanted it. For nearly a decade now she had been defining herself by her loathing for him. And if he were gone, who would she be, if not the sick, miserable soul that hated Dan? She needed him.

For so long, she'd treated her marriage as a prison. But now that she realized that she actually, physically, wasn't in a prison, that she was free, the freedom itself terrified her. Because if there weren't any limits, than she wasn't safe. All the limits and boundaries she'd imposed on herself— to brush her teeth every morning, to not drown her children when they were driving her crazy, to say hello to people she knew when walking by them on the street—were just that: self-imposed. In reality, Karen thought, the only real limit to one's collection of behaviors was death.

She hadn't called Peter. She decided to go to the bar and see if he was there. She peeked inside: he wasn't there. She began walking to a church in Carroll Gardens. It was a Wednesday night, and she used to go to a meeting there, in the basement.

In the parlance of those who go to AA meetings, it was not a "good" meeting. Tom, and others—the Harvard girl, for instance—had explained that some meetings were "good". Or rather, some meetings contained more hipsters, better conversation, and took place in nicer spaces. All meetings had names—Ninth Step, One Day at A Time, Agnostics for A.A., Lesbians and Gays for Sobriety, and so forth. This Wednesday meeting in Carroll Gardens was called Spirit of the Universe.

She stopped off at a bodega and bought a bottle of water and some menthol coughdrops. It started to rain. She arrived a bit late, and hurrying because of the rain, she nearly fell on the cement steps as she entered through a side door of the large, dark stone Catholic Church. Down into the basement she went. It was cool and gray, a bit damp. It smelled funny, just as she remembered it. It was, in a word, bleak. There was none of the cheer and good fashion that existed at other meetings.

Sitting in a circle on rickety metal chairs were three people, the same three people who were there the last time she was there months before. This made her eyes fill. God, she thought, what a beautiful thing. A horrible, naked bulb hung from a wire in the ceiling. Karen stumbled in. She got a chair and pulled it up. Everyone scooted around, scraping the chairs on the cement floor, making room for her. Why, Karen wondered, were they relegated to this nasty hole, when above, was a beautiful empty church? Because they were all in some sort of hell? Or was it purgatory, this smelly, unkind basement?

A heavy, dark-haired woman who appeared Italian and in her late forties led the group. Indeed, it was her group and Karen remembered her appearing self-conscious and defensive at the general failure of it—it wasn't popular, it wasn't fun. Her name was Mary, and she was an alcoholic. She had been sober for nearly a decade, that Karen remembered, too. And she was on many psychotropic drugs—Prozac, sleeping pills, etc...The last time Karen had been there, she spoke about switching from one thing to another, from Prozac to Zoloft, or something like that.

Karen still felt boozy. A spasm of panic struck her. What was she doing here? She was drunk!

"Welcome back, Karen," Mary said, smiling in that way people smile who are heavily medicated.

She passed the basket around and Karen put in a five dollar bill in it out of guilt.

"Welcome back," the two men chimed in. One was also in his late forties, white and wearing a very prim striped shirt with a bow tie. The other man was black and he had the nods. Karen knew what the nods were. She had worked at a bar in the East Village before she was married and there were a couple of junkies who would shoot up in the bathroom and then nod out over their drinks.

"You want to go first, Percival? Let's all just take turns talking, OK?" Mary said, smiling still, her lips stretched nervously against her teeth.

"I think I'll pass for now," he said. "I worked a late shift. I'm very tired. I want to listen first."

"Well alright then. James? Would you go first?" Mary held the basket in her lap. She was sitting up very straight.

James was happy to go first. He loved to talk and he had much to talk about. In particular, he enjoyed sharing his anguish over his witch of a daughter, who at the age of thirteen, was in the process of getting a court order against him. She was legally ending their visits, because she accused him of physical and sexual abuse. "I'm just so angry," he said. "My rage at her is consuming me. I am trying to let God and let go, because I can't do anything about it that I know. But it's killing me. I want to strangle her." He made a strangling motion with his hands. He looked like a professor at a New England boarding school but Karen remembered that he was a disbarred lawyer.

Suddenly, it all made sense to her, her being here. "I'm drunk," Karen blurted out. "I've been drinking."

"Oh," Mary said, and then put a hand to her mouth. One wasn't supposed to talk until the sharing was over. It was a rule.

"I like drinking," Karen continued. "I like the release. I like the relaxing effect. The numbing effect. I don't want to black out anymore. I just want to drink and not drink too much."

"I know I'm not supposed to say anything until the meeting is over, but I do want to point out that one of the premises of AA is that it is a progressive illness. Your drinking is not going to get better. It will only get worse and then it will kill you," Mary said.

"And what are you going to die from? We all are going to die. No matter how many meetings we go to, we are going to die. Is death such a failure? Does how we die matter?"

Percival, with much effort, lifted his head and through a very dry mouth encrusted with what looked like white sand, said, "It does. How we die. How we live. It does matter."

"But you are *high*. I know you are. You are high on smack." Karen said, throwing up her hands. "That is not a lovely way to go, ODing on heroin."

"Oh, my," said Mary. "I think we have broken the AA rules here. It's my fault. I started it by saying something. And I'm sorry."

Percival looked at Karen. "*Bitch*, I'm not high."

"Fuck you! You are *so* high!"

"Karen, I am going to have to ask you to leave." Mary said. "You are welcome back when you are not drinking, OK? We'd love to have you back. We'll pray for you. We'll pray for you every time we end the meeting. But you have to leave."

Karen got up. A child molester, a heroin addict and a seriously depressed pharmaceutical junkie were going to pray for her. This made her cry, made her soul sing with sorrow and joy. "Thank you. Thank you for praying for me."

When she got home, Dan was sitting on the couch in the living room, with a light on, reading the newspaper.

"Please don't go downstairs right away. We need to talk."

She sat down across from him, with her coat and shoes still on. Dan didn't know how to talk. It was on her list of the many things she hated about him. There was silence. Then he said, "How are you?"

"How am I? What the fuck is that? Some office greeting? *How are you*? Good Lord, save me."

He looked crestfallen. For a fleeting second, she felt sorry for him. Then it passed.

"Let me try again," he said, and sighed. "How was your evening?"

"Go to hell."

"Listen. We have to think about the children."

"Think about the children? You fucking think about the children. Your kids barely know you. "

"You can't drink like this. Think about the children, really. They need you."

"You've lost me here, Dan. You don't even have to show up for dinner more than twice a week and you tell me to think about the children?"

"I want you to stop sleeping with this other man."

"You and I don't have sex."

Dan looked away, not that he was ever quite looking at Karen. He seemed to have been staring at something very important at the tip of his long, aristocratic nose and now he had pointed it elsewhere.

"What do you do," Karen asked, "If you're not fucking someone else? Masturbate?"

His eyes crossed slightly and his face colored every so delicately. He was not, by any means, a hot-tempered man. "Stop it, Karen."

"Oh, I'm sorry Dan. Did I offend you? Does the word *masturbate* offend you?"

Dan stood. "You've lost control. I don't know what to do. I might call the police."

"*Call the police?*"

"You're drunk and out of control..."

"Because I used the word *masturbate*?"

"I'm going to have you committed to a rehabilitation center." Dan stood and walked over to the phone. Karen followed him and knocked the phone out of his hand.

"Fuck you! I'll call the police on you! You treat me like your house slave, like your fucking *nigger*, and you're going to call the police on me?"

"Stop! Just stop it! Don't talk like that!"

"Oh, now it's the word *nigger* that upsets you? *Nigger! Nigger nigger nigger!*"

"You're doing this just to be hateful to me." Dan sat again and put his head in his hands. "I don't know what to do. I'm sorry. I'm sorry I haven't been a very good husband."

It was as if a storm had subsided, the mood so quickly deflated. All the rage was gone. Was it the power of remorse? What was left was pity and sorrow and a hollowness that made Karen's breath disappear.

"Don't be sorry," said Karen. "I have people *praying* for me. Did you know that? I have people praying for me. I'm just glad we had this talk. I'm going to go out now. But we can talk more later. Maybe about getting a divorce. I don't know."

She got on the F train and headed for 2nd Avenue. In the East Village, where she used to work, no one knew her anymore. The bar had changed owners. The crowd seemed impossibly young. Had she ever been this young? Could that have been? She drank until dawn. In the early morning, she took a cab back home. Driving over the Brooklyn Bridge, the sun shone translucent yellow off the ships in the East River and the tall, many-windowed buildings surrounding the water. It was the beginning of another day and the world was a beautiful, glorious place, despite the cement and garbage, the oil in the river, the pain and suffering of its people and animals. It made her think of God. The world held such magic, and yet, she had ruined her life. Made a mess of it. She had hoped Dan would save her. Then her kids. But children and husbands don't save their mothers or wives, not in Karen's world. No one person can save another.

She remembered a fight she'd had with Dan, years ago, before she quit drinking, before she started again.

"You are so angry with me, because you don't love me." She had said, boldly, looking at him intently, wanting to see it wasn't so.

"What?"

"You think it's my fault you don't love me. You are angry that I am not lovable, that I don't inspire your love."

"That's ridiculous. You're crazy. You're acting like a crazy person." He said, but his face gave it away. It was the truth. It shocked him. Drinking had never been the problem, Karen realized. It was not believing the truths it revealed.

It was silly, to be upset about this. Or anything. Disappointment was just a part of life, of everyone's life. And yet she wondered, what would she do now? Go have another drink? It seemed the only answer.

SHE WAS EVERYTHING TO HIM

Does that make you wet? Jon had wanted to say, to spit at her, when he got home from work the night before, at eight o'clock. There she was, on the couch, droopy sweatpants around her still round belly, cradling their son at her breast. No music playing, no TV on, just the soft slurping noise of their three-year-old son Frank nursing from his wife's breast. He had said nothing. He'd said plenty in the past and done plenty in the past and nothing got through to her. Marie just didn't give a shit.

No, he said nothing at all to her after letting himself into their house, nothing rude or confrontational, nor anything nice. There was no evening greeting at his house. He walked in, and neither his wife nor his son raised their head to acknowledge the fact. Such was Jon's life. His son, his boy, did not jump off the couch and run to him, saying, "Daddy, daddy!" Jon's co-workers talked about the greetings their children gave them when they returned home in the evenings. Jon would pretend he knew what they were talking about. But things were different in his home. Frank didn't run to see him when he walked in. Not ever. Was there a time, when Frank was a tiny infant, that Marie had let him hold his son for awhile when he came home? There was. There must have been. But it was so long ago.

Yes, last night had been, in many ways, a night like any other. A disappointment, a belittlement. Tonight, there was nothing left for Jon to do at his desk. His desk was so free of clutter he knew people thought he was anal. But what else could he do but work non-stop? Where else was he needed? After ceremoniously wiping his hand across the wide expanse of wood veneer that was his desk, his hand picking up particles of fine, white dust, Jon left work—he was a project coordinator at a small industrial design firm—and walked to a bar in the deep of Hell's Kitchen. The walk took thirty minutes, upward and westward and he enjoyed it, enjoyed walking in the wrong direction from home. The bar, where he'd become quite a regular, was a dirty, friendly place. The TV was always on, but it was relatively quiet. No one bothered you if you wanted to sit there and stare into your drink and be left alone. Or you could talk about sports or politics with the old Irish guy tending bar, or talk to some other old alcoholic sitting there watching TV alongside you. It was a place where Jon liked the choices. All of the choices felt good. He ordered a beer and a shot of whiskey and stared into his beer.

Last night, he'd fucked his wife and she hadn't wanted him to. But he did anyway. It was the first time in six months that they'd had marital relations. Six months ago, they'd kissed and cuddled and he fondled her and she seemed so annoyed, laying there putting up with him, with her head turned toward the wall. This had hurt him deeply, and yet he continued to kiss her, to make love to her. Six months ago, he'd *felt* as if he were raping his wife, even though she made no vocal protest and he did everything he could to show his love and affection for her. But she just didn't care about him anymore. Christ, they used to make love twice a week! She used to turn toward him, wrapping her soft body around his, her long, pale brown hair getting tangled in his face and arms. There had been so much love for him, so much tenderness. Where had it gone? When did she stop loving him? Was it true, did she not love him at all anymore? Jon was afraid to ask. He was afraid she'd look at him as she so often did now, her eyes so angry, so distant, and say, I don't love you anymore. And so he didn't ask. Because he felt he couldn't handle the truth.

For six months, he hadn't tried to approach her. He hoped, wrongfully as he now knew, that she would approach him when she was ready to make room for him again. But she never was ready. She didn't seem to need his touch anymore. She was always touching Frank and Frank was always touching her and perhaps this was why, and yet it didn't make complete sense. Frank was three! Once, she had loved Jon's arms wrapped around her. Once, he had made her feel safe and protected. He knew that he'd had that effect on her, he did. Now, what was it? That being a mother made her feel so strong? So self-reliant? That their son, a fucking three-year-old for God's sake, gave her everything she needed? He'd tried talking with her. "Maybe we should get a babysitter and go out to dinner." he'd said. She looked at him like he was crazy. And then, one lazy Sunday morning, while he read the paper and she nursed and cuddled Frank, he said, "Maybe Frank should go to pre-school a few hours a week, so you could have some time to yourself."

"I don't need any time to myself," she said. Then, abruptly: "I'm going to Danielle's house for a playdate." And off she went. As if the very mention of not being with Frank was so awful that she had to leave Jon there at home, alone, on the weekend, the one time when they really could be together. He was not needed, not wanted. He had given his sperm to Marie and now she was done with him. That's what it felt like.

He thought about saying, I miss you, but he was too ashamed. He thought about bringing up marriage counseling, but again, he was too ashamed. Wasn't she the one who was supposed to do that? At first, during his morning showers, he masturbated efficiently. Then he began having fewer and fewer erections. It was like his libido was dormant. His body had been so unloved and untouched for so long, that his essence, his inner life, the thing that made him feel like a person, just died. Now he was just despair and rage, despair and rage.

When they'd first been together, all those years ago, he remembered his head between her breasts, how he'd said "Thank you."

"For what?" she asked quietly, stroking his head.

"For giving my life joy and meaning." he answered her.

Last night, when he fucked her, he'd been incredibly angry. The rage took over and it almost felt good and it definitively felt unlike the depression that often was like a thick cloud around his weeks. The depression felt like nothing, a heavy, endless nothing, and nothing was death. But fucking her last night had not been nothing. It had been something, at the very least, it had been something. Their son Frank lay asleep in bed with them like always, curled up against Marie. This sleeping arrangement was another thing that Jon had given up on trying to change. And so, last night, while his son gurgled his soft child's breath in bed with them Jon stuck his hand between his wife's teeth, another hand grabbing her flabby ass, and he fucked her from behind without a care for how dry she was, without caring how she bit his hand and made small noises of protest. Fuck her. Fuck Frank, fuck her, fuck the both of them. As he thrust his dick into her dry cunt he thought, I'm raping my wife, I'm raping my wife. He came very quickly. He rolled over and fell asleep immediately in his own bed. He'd been sleeping on the couch for which seemed like forever. It was the first night he'd slept in his own bed in months—or longer?—and he slept a black, solid mass of sleep.

On Frank's second birthday, after they blew out two candles and sang him Happy Birthday, Jon had put his arm around Marie and whispered "Let's have another." It had only been a year ago when Jon still had certain hopes.

Marie had hissed, "Frank is still a baby! I'm just not ready yet."

Now, a year later, Jon felt sure Marie would never be ready. There was going to be no family. There was Marie and Frank, and then there was Jon.

His hopes were dashed. His vision of the future—a future with two or three kids, a loving wife, vacations by the beach—no longer seemed viable. Where there once was a loving wife, there now was a ghost of sorts. He had once hoped that her hostility and aloofness were a phase, something that would have a life of its own and then disappear, back to wherever it came from. But Jon no longer dreamed that Marie's hostility would go away. As he saw it now, it wasn't that certain emotions took over Marie, but rather that she herself had changed permanently and was to remain a forever altered person. Marie was now a slightly fat, cranky, scowling housewife and a neurotic and overly-attached mother. She was not the woman he married. He married someone earthy, for sure. He married a woman who was most comfortable in jeans and a loose sweater, who rarely wore more makeup than a bit of lipstick. But Marie had also been easy to laugh, sharp-witted and full of joy and mischievousness. She'd loved movies and parties. She had been earthy, but fun; practical, but not entirely unsophisticated. Gone, gone. All of that was gone.

Had the problems first appeared when she got pregnant with Frank? It had been a hard, stressful pregnancy. No, it was before that, when they first started to try for a baby, because she'd had two miscarriages before the conception of Frank. The first miscarriage was hugely disappointing for both of them. They wanted children badly, they did, and they were giddy like children themselves when they found out she was pregnant. But they'd been able to comfort each other through that loss. Trying to get Marie pregnant again, after the first miscarriage, had been a delicate and loaded affair. She'd been so vulnerable to him. It had been beautiful, too, making love to his fragile wife. And God, he'd been so gentle with her.

After the second miscarriage, the bitter, hard look first surfaced, the one that now permanently resided on Marie's face. Hardness took away her beauty, transformed her physical features into sharp unapproachable things, and yet he still loved her, wanted her and her only, for himself. He'd never loved anyone besides Marie. He'd never really lusted after any other woman and this was something that embarrassed him. She was everything to him. Looking back, Jon now realized that after the second miscarriage was when things had really started to go wrong.

Christ, it was as if the world had ended. You'd think she was the only woman in the world who'd had two miscarriages. And Jon had been disappointed, too. After the first one, he, too, had been able to be sad, had been given the room to show his emotions. They had been there for each other for that one. After the second miscarriage, he tried to console her, to reach out to her, but now she brushed him off. He'd said, "It's gonna be OK, Marie. Your doctor says you're fine, we're just having some bad luck. Nothing is wrong with you, remember that. You're all checked out and you're fine, OK?"

"I'm not fine and nothing's OK. You try having a clump of bloody cells come out of you. A fucking liver. I gave birth to a small liver. You try having that happen to you twice. I want a baby, dammit! And this is what my body gives me. You try failing at the only thing that matters. Then you can talk."

"Why are you angry with me? It's not my fault."

She stormed out. He stood there, his arms open wide to an empty room.

When she was ready to try again, she let him know. At night, completely naked in bed next to him, she'd put her hands on his shoulders. But she was all business, he could tell, although he tried fooling himself into thinking she was loving him, giving to him, enjoying herself. He needed to believe everything was OK. But it wasn't. They had sex like clockwork, for a few days every month during that time when she was fertile. Jon was desperate for her, for feeling close to her, and so he tried to fool himself. But she gave nothing of herself to him, and just took what he gave her. Then, when she got pregnant, how happy he was! Marie, though, wouldn't even let him hug her. "Don't, I don't feel well," and she pushed him off.

"Sweetheart, I'm so happy and this one is gonna stick. I just know it." He'd said.

"I don't know it. Nor do you. No one knows anything."

That was it. After that, he couldn't touch her. The pregnancy did stick, their son was born, there was supposed to be so much joy. But Marie had stopped being Marie. Even the birth of Frank couldn't bring her back. Indeed, their son took her further away from him than he ever thought was possible. He'd tried to be happy and he tried to be patient. But now, three years later, he couldn't try anything anymore.

Now, nothing was OK. Now, there was no pretending. He had raped his fucking wife last night. For years now, God, for more years than not, they'd been miserable.

The bar began filling a bit. Some older, white-haired and purple-nosed working class men sat on stools and drank. Jon ordered another beer and another shot. A woman came in, one he'd seen before but never spoken to. She was short, squattish, with badly dyed hair that frizzled in a bad perm around her head. She looked to be in her forties, but could be twenty-nine. Jon always assumed she was a hooker and a drug addict. It was Hell's Kitchen after all, and he was in a dive bar. People were friendly to her, but not Jon. He tried not to look at her; she was that hideous to him. And yet, he knew her jeans and the rolls of flesh above her hips. He knew she drank whiskey and ginger ale. Was this his future? Sitting in vile bars, noticing, against his will, the habits and bodies of decrepit whores?

It was dark outside when Jon left. The air was beautiful. Garbage swirled on the streets like tiny ghosts. The sky was like an enormous Christmas tree, lit with bright pinpricks from the windows of all the buildings in midtown. He descended into the subway to head back home to Park Slope, Brooklyn. Even at this hour, at nearly nine o'clock, the train was full of people returning home from work. Jon, of course, was drunk, his long face red and hot. There were women everywhere, young women, middle-aged women, carrying briefcases and wearing shining shoes. In the horrible fluorescent glow of the train, they appeared to him like candy, beautifully wrapped candy made just for a holiday. And yet, he didn't want any of them. He just wanted his wife. He just wanted Marie. She was the only person who was real to him and he knew he lacked the imagination necessary to see his way to anyone else. She was the one thing in life that was life to him, and she'd taken herself away. All that was left were whores and false, doll-like professionals with the bodies of mannequins.

In Park Slope, as he approached their brownstone, he noticed the lights were off downstairs and upstairs. He assumed Marie and Frank were already asleep, huddled together, breathing the same air. He opened the door carefully, looking into the dark entranceway of his house. The stroller lay neatly folded up against the wall. An array of coats and hats hung forlornly on hooks. Jon listened, his head cocked up toward the stairs, up to where the bedrooms were, but he only heard the slight noise from the street—a passing car, a quiet voice. His house was utterly void of noise. Jon, still outside, closed the door quietly and locked it and walked back down his steps. He looked at his dark building, his house, the one he was so proud of owning. This was not his home anymore. At the corner of his block, lowering his head to protect himself from the wind, he turned left on Seventh Avenue and kept going. What had she said to him that night? After he rolled himself off of her, after he removed his throbbing hand from her teeth? She'd said something. She must have said something really important.

IF THERE WERE TWO BOATS

He was not Edie's favorite son. Regardless, it pained her that he married such a woman and lived such a life. Her favorite son, Thomas, lived in Los Angeles and was a very successful producer and had been divorced twice. She loved visiting Thomas—he lived in an enormous house near the beach in Santa Monica and had tons of staff and there was no horrible daughter-in-law to ruin things. Thomas usually took Edie out for an expensive, fabulous dinner (almost always there was a movie star, or television star at the restaurant, it was so fun, so silly, but so fun) and then, the rest of the time in LA—Edie almost always went for a long weekend—she visited with an old friend from Smith who'd lived there forever and her half sister, Veronica. Visiting Thomas was just pure joy! The sun, the wonderful surroundings, the nice dinners (and gifts, too: jewelry, a piece of furniture that he'd have shipped to her). Perhaps it was true that she wished he'd meet someone with whom to share his life. The only thing was that Thomas didn't seem as if he were missing anything or anyone, for that matter, and so it was hard to worry about him. He was rich, he loved his work, and he had some good friends, interesting, successful friends, (even a few of those aforementioned movie stars, which Edie thought was just wonderfully amusing and great). The two women he married had been more trouble than they were worth and he'd figured that out quickly. Maybe that was the problem, women today. Women today were just dreadful, or so it seemed. He was smart, her Thomas. And handsome. He'd always been her smarter and more handsome boy.

Michael, on the other hand, still lived nearby. Well, sort of. He lived in Brooklyn. She lived upstate, in Millbrook, in a six bedroom house, well off of any road, on eighty acres. After her husband died, she sold the apartment on the East Side and moved to the country permanently. This was hard on Michael. Thomas, of course, didn't care one way or the other. Why would he care? He was in LA; he had his own life and worries. Michael (this was before he married) called twice a week, came out almost every weekend, and fretted over her. She was fine. He, apparently, was not, but the charade was that she was out there alone and he had to come visit his poor old lonely mother. The weekend visits became such a drag (he was there for her to cook for him and to wash the dishes afterward, despite his whining on about how he worried about her being isolated, lonely, etc...) that finally she had to put an end to them. She did that by always being at *least* twenty minutes late to pick him up from the train station, by scheduling dinners and lunches with friends (that eliminated the meals for him) and by not changing the sheets in the guest room, ever, even when the whole room began to smell, frankly, disgusting. Finally, Michael stopped coming out every weekend (although he still came out). And then he got married.

This was all six years ago. He married so quickly. She was from Minnesota and spoke using a horrific, Midwestern dialect—all drawn out vowels and dangling participles and strange non-words and mispronunciations. She had small eyes and a large, obscene mouth. A country girl. A Midwesterner, with dubious schooling from some state university. She was...she was beyond disappointing. She was not a small girl, not petite like Edie herself. She struck Edie as truly unappealing. She was, in every respect, unsuitable for her son. Even her least favorite son, the one who cried too much as an infant, the one who was uncoordinated, who needed glasses, who clung to her as a boy too big to be clinging to his mother, who had terrible acne as a teenager. Yes, not even for Michael, the son she never understood or even liked very much, although he was her son, and there was something there, some sort of maternal feeling. He was her son! He was something to her.

His wife's name was Jane. He met her at work, when he still worked in publishing (he'd since moved onto the Internet world). They eloped, which was a relief for Edie, because the last thing she wanted was to "celebrate" this union or be forced to buy expensive tickets to Minnesota. Or have to talk to Jane's low-class (let's just be honest), Midwestern family. After they married, they moved to Park Slope, Brooklyn, which Edie was sure to be the end of the world. Brooklyn! Good lord, her ancestors were rolling over in their graves. Yet, truthfully, Park Slope wasn't so bad. And this was a relief to Edie. She hadn't known what to expect and she didn't want a horrible life for Michael. She didn't. She didn't want to be ashamed of him.

She had visited them only twice. That was enough. They visited her every few months for awhile there, which was better than her trying to navigate herself around Brooklyn; she preferred to see them in Millbrook. She visited them the first time because Jane had recently gotten pregnant. It all happened so quickly—the marriage, the pregnancy—and that wasn't a good thing, of course. Having children is so stressful, it's such a huge event, and it's always better to have been married for awhile first. Get to know one another, get over the disappointments that a marriage inevitably brings, and God knows in their marriage there had to be a lot of those.

Jane, during her pregnancy, had gained enormous amounts of weight. In Edie's day, her doctor wouldn't have let her get away with that. Jane didn't have a doctor, she had something called a midwife, whatever that was, and when Edie remarked on how quickly Jane had gotten so big (she still had her manners, she tried to address the subject in a polite, roundabout sort of way), Jane answered that her midwife had said to eat as much as she wanted to. Then there was her son during that visit. Sitting on a drab, sagging beige couch, something they'd bought used, they told her excitedly, which of course dismayed Edie. Used tables, used lamps, yes, of course, but a used couch? Disgusting. And that was the word for so much of Michael's life. His wife disgusted her, their couch disgusted her, the smell—sour and musty, with some choking potpourri stink layered on top—in their apartment disgusted her. And there Michael sat on that visit, across the small room, directly across from her, next to his enormous and hideous wife. Michael, who'd never been a pretty sight, was now a solid thirty pounds overweight.

"It happens sometimes, we've talked to people about it," he said about his weight gain.

"We've talked to our therapist about it," Jane clarified, much to Edie's embarrassment. "It's a sympathy thing. It's normal, healthy even. Sometimes the husband gains weight and gets indigestion, just like his pregnant wife. It'll all go away when the baby arrives."

"Well I've never heard of such a thing. I'm just concerned about your diet. Your cholesterol and such. Remember your father's heart condition. You just need to take care of yourself."

"Don't worry Mom. Jane and I are taking care of ourselves."

"We are! We just rest a lot and because we are more sedentary, we're gaining weight, that's all. Rest is very important when we're pregnant." Jane added.

"I see. Well I ate like a bird when I was pregnant and smoked a lot so as not to eat too much. I always had a cigarette in my mouth!"

"You could nearly get arrested for that nowadays. Smoking is terrible for the fetus. It can cause miscarriage." Jane's beady eyes focused right on her.

"Well, clearly it didn't in my case. How's work?" She tried to change the subject.

"Work's fine. Jane quit her job. We want her to be home with the baby."

Now it was Edie's turn to look straight at her daughter-in-law. "Can you afford to quit now? Why not wait until maternity leave and then quit? I mean, money is money, no?" This had just made Edie nervous. Michael would never be Thomas, that she knew. But the last thing she wanted was them borrowing money from her. Or worse, sinking deeper into a shabby lifestyle. She just couldn't bear things getting any worse than they were.

"We're fine, mom. We don't need much right now. Right now the baby matters. We'll worry about money later."

That was the end for Edie. She just stopped trying after that. Worrying about the baby is worrying about money and if they didn't know that, then she didn't understand them at all. At all. End of discussion.

Oh, the mystery that is life. The mystery of our own blood, of the thing we carried, or carry, inside of ourselves. And yet we endure. She wished Thomas had given her a grandchild with one of his wives. That child would have lived in a great big sunny room, would have had young au pairs looking after him, and would have gone to the best schools in LA. She had asked Thomas once if he wanted children. She had even gone so far as to suggest that he should have a child. He'd said no. Children were not part of his "plan". Fair enough for him. But the grandchild she didn't have was more fun to think about than the grandchild she did have.

A granddaughter. And here was the truth—she never wanted a daughter, she never had a daughter and she was slightly put off by this grandchild being a girl. (A four-year-old girl, at this time). They named her after Edie. She knew she should have been grateful. And she was flattered, if nothing else, for a moment. But she also was...distressed. She didn't want to have Michael's child named after her. She didn't want that. Not Michael's child.

The day the baby was born, Michael called her from the hospital. She was excited for them and flattered and yet, there was something in Michael's voice. Something so needy. Even after marriage. Even now that he was a father. He was trying to make her happy, that was how she felt— Look here! I have a baby for you!—and it reminded her of when he was an eight-year-old boy and he would draw her picture after picture and she would pretend to like them (he was no artist). He'd say, "Mommy, won't you hang it up in your room? I made it just for you." And she'd say, "Yes I will! Not right this minute, but later I will." And later, after Michael went to bed, she'd throw the pictures away. One day, she was coming down the hall of their apartment and heading to put away some new shoes in her closet and Michael stood there, in her room, looking at the empty walls (there was of course, a lovely small, early Matisse that she'd inherited from her mother) with a sullen face. "What are you doing in here? I don't like you in my room. Go on!" She said, as she chased him out. The look he gave her. Edie was not prone to guilt, but it was a fierce look. He stopped making her pictures after that. After that, he made pictures for his second grade teacher.

Michael had invited Edie to the hospital but she declined and said she'd rather wait until they got back to Park Slope and then she'd visit. Her daughter-in-law's birth had been a hard one—not that she really needed to know, but there you have it, that was how they were, no proper manners regarding anything. All this therapy! Therapy this, therapy that. And to talk about it! To talk about everything. What Jane needed was a class in social etiquette, not anymore damn therapy. She needed to learn to talk only after she'd finished chewing, she needed to learn how to sit up straight, she needed to learn how not to scowl if she felt like scowling—one doesn't display all emotions whenever one feels like it, dammit!—she needed to learn how to be less of a rude beast. But no, it was more and more therapy,

until any semblance of a proper, controlled life
had disappeared. Jane and Michael were either in
therapy or in their foul apartment, talking about
therapy. Edie just tried not to think about them.
But that was hard. It was hard not to think about
them.

Michael had never been a manly sort of young
man, but now, it seemed, his wife had sucked out
every last remaining bit of male integrity he had
had. Jane, without a doubt, emasculated him and
turned him into a spineless, beaten down, soft
eunuch. Damn her.

And so after the baby was home, Edie visited
them again. The curtains were filthy and the
house smelled like dirty diapers. Michael and
Jane were ecstatic and delirious. Edie vaguely
remembered those feelings when Thomas had
been born. She and her husband had been giddy
and overwhelmed and, well, it was quite a
moment, the birth of your first child. Edie brought
a bottle of champagne, but they refused to drink
it.

"Oh, no, Mom. Thanks. But we're not drinking
because Jane is breastfeeding and it's just not a
good idea."

"Well for goodness sake Michael, you're not,
ah, nursing. Why don't you have a glass with me?
I have a grandchild! I want to celebrate."

"Ah, no, Mom. I can't. It wouldn't be fair to
Jane."

Now was the time for Jane to say, You go
ahead! Or something to that effect. But no.

Nothing. She sat there on their couch, without even offering Edie a seat, still hugely fat, and she lifted her soggy-looking gray T-shirt and pulled out an enormous drooping breast, and placed the baby right on it.

"Oh my, Jane, would you like some privacy? Michael and I can go in the kitchen..." Edie was taken aback. She couldn't not look, but she didn't want to look, either. She was repulsed but felt compelled to steal glances, like at a car wreck.

"There's no reason for you two to leave the room," Jane said, fixing her steely little eyes on Edie. She had such a way with glaring right at you.

When Edie thought of her marriage she remembered fondly all that had not been said. She remembered the modesty, the grace of their lives together. All that had been assumed or understood. She thought of how late at night, her husband would do things to her, in the darkness of their room. How he would not so gently grasp her neck or push her face down. But always, in the daylight, in the rooms where people gathered, fully dressed and awake, there had always been such decorum.

That was the last visit. Edie stayed standing and finally Michael asked her to sit down in an armchair and she did and Michael jabbered on about the birth. The episiotomy, the deep moaning, the blood. My God! Edie nearly fainted. "Excuse me," she said, and went into the bathroom. The bathroom, of course, was musty and damp and dirty. Little, dark, slimy hairs clung to the sink and the toilet seat was up, revealing a stained, vile bowl of water. She shut it and sat down on the lid. She tried to steady herself. It would all be over soon. This visit, this moment. Like the moment of infancy that Michael and Jane were experiencing; the visit was feeling endless, monumental, and just like the moment of infancy, it felt like the most important thing that could ever be. But really, in hindsight, abruptly, it's over. Just like that. Like waking from a dream that felt so real it takes awhile to shake the feeling that it wasn't. Edie stood to go out, feeling better. She'd say her good-byes and head back to Millbrook. And as she got up to leave she saw a sweater of hers hanging on a hook on the bathroom door. A blue cashmere sweater, one she'd bought years ago at Saks and had left in the guest room to be used on a chilly spring morning by guests, if they needed something. But there it was. Jane had taken it, without asking. How could Jane fit into that sweater? There was no way, really. Edie picked it up, determined for one moment to bring it back with her. Then, just as quickly, she changed her mind. She put it back on the hook, and opened the door to leave.

That was the last time she went to Park Slope. After that they came out to Millbrook, with the baby, about once a month. And then, eventually, even those visits stopped. When the child was almost a year old, Michael had called her. Yes, it was after that phone call that the monthly visits stopped. She now saw them on Thanksgiving. And Memorial Day. Twice a year, for the day only. They stayed at an inn nearby and left the next morning. Twice a year was just right.

He had called her from work, one Friday afternoon. He called her looking for something she couldn't give him.

"Mom," he'd said, his voice so pained that she closed her eyes so as to try and not imagine the sorrow on his face, "Every night she calls and asks me to come home NOW. It'll be five in the evening and no one leaves at five, no one, and other people have kids too, you know. And she sounds as if she's having a breakdown. She goes on and on about how she can't take it. How she needs me to come home. And I'll hear Edie crying in the background and it makes me nervous so I leave. I come home. And when I arrive, little Edie will be happy in her highchair, with food smeared all over her, and Jane will be lovingly spooning some homemade baby food into her."

"Well, what do you say her to her then?" she asked her son.

"She does most of the talking. She thanks me profusely for coming home. She cries a bit sometimes. But everything seems OK by the time I get home. So I did ask her once, or say to her, you know, everything seems OK by the time I get home. And she said, everything *is* OK, *because* you're home. "

"Well, are you worried about being fired?"

"I don't know." Silence. A heavy sigh.

"You need to get her a nanny, or at least some kind of part-time help."

"I brought that up once, but she said no. She refused completely." Sigh. "She just wants me around. She's become so demanding."

"Jane was always demanding, sweetheart." Edie said, enjoying it as it came out, even though she knew it was a mistake.

"That's not what I want to hear from you, Mom."

"Well then, Michael, don't talk to me about your wife if you don't want me to at least agree with you about her."

"Who else can I talk to, Mom?" And his voice was entirely cracked now. He was all but sobbing. Her son, her grown son, reduced to this. Was it her fault? "I can't talk to her and if I can't talk to you, then who am I to turn to?"

"Weren't you in therapy? Can't you talk to your therapist?"

"We were in couple's therapy. The therapist was always on her side. I always felt disliked by that woman. And you hated that I was in therapy, remember?"

So God help her. Of course she hated that her son was in therapy. For one, it was because his wife was a castrating bitch, and also, it didn't make her feel good about the job she'd done with Michael. But now she was just angry and fed up.

"Listen to you! What I think about therapy, what your wife wants you to do? You need to be your own person, Michael, and I fear I can't help you anymore with that. And I just don't think I'm the one you should be calling with your marriage problems. Why don't you call your brother, or a friend?"

"I have no friends. Not good friends. I only have work acquaintances, really."

"So call Thomas! For God's sake! Don't you get it? I can't teach you how to be a man! I'm not one!" And then she hung up on him. He would never call Thomas; they were not close, and they never had been. But what else was she to do? Michael, the one she ignored more than pampered, the one she could never look at with true love in her eyes because Thomas was her true love, and after that, well, it had probably been her husband. And after that? She had never appreciated Michael, if for no other reason than she didn't understand what he was. He was, and always had been, completely foreign to her. A stranger, walking around her house and trying to climb up on her lap. How is it that he came *from* her? An alien creature. A foreigner. A strange little boy looking at her so fiercely, so relentlessly, trying to suck something from her eyes that wasn't there. What else *could* she do? She would look away. It was her only gift to him, to try and save him from the truth. Because not all mothers love all of their children. Why God made it so, Edie did not know. And actually, looking away all those years had not been her only gift. But it had been a start to a long line of them. Because even if she was not given any love for him, she had made him hers and hers only. If she could not love him, she could still have him. In many ways, more than she had Thomas. Because now, when she saw Michael and his wife and their child on Thanksgiving, or at the end of May, when the sun is just starting to warm things up, she saw that he did not really love his wife. Love had nothing to do with building a life, this Edie knew, of course. Michael would build a life with Jane, a life built around their child. He was with Jane, he obeyed her still, of that Edie was nearly certain, but he did not truly love her. Indeed, that was most likely why he married her. She was no threat. He had married someone who wouldn't disturb his relationship with his mother. He was always going to be Edie's and Edie's only. If there were two boats, one with Edie going in one direction and another with Jane and their daughter going in the opposite direction, and Michael had to make a choice, a final choice, he would jump into Edie's boat. Of this, Edie was certain.

How strange, that a lack of love can be more binding than love itself. She hadn't meant it to be so. But she wasn't in control of everything, was she?

BABY

Lara had some ambitions, admittedly vague ones
—to publish some poems, to throw great parties—
but it was true that she had always wanted a baby.
There came a time in her late twenties when she
quit working at *The New Yorker* so she could
teach pre-school. This was a pre-baby maneuver.
Then, finally, her longstanding boyfriend Robert
proposed (after much prodding, but who cares?—
it was over and done with) and she quit teaching
pre-school to plan her wedding. Being married
and having a baby was how she had always
imagined herself, and suddenly, here it all was!
She bought a huge loft downtown—Robert didn't
make a lot of money, but she had an enormous
trust fund—and set up house. A new, eight
thousand dollar couch! A Sub-Zero refrigerator! A
handmade rug from Tibet! And, most importantly,
a specially designed room for the baby. Because
shortly after the wedding, she announced to
Robert that they would no longer be using birth
control. A baby! All to herself! At parties, she
gravitated toward the babies. She cooed and
gurgled at them, and occasionally—she couldn't
help herself—aggressively relieved the mother of
her pudgy little charge, and bounced and cuddled
the baby. Little, helpless children! Oh, how their
mothers often failed them. During her stint as a
pre-school teacher, she'd try to repair the damage

done. She loved children, she did, she did, she did.

After taking her temperature religiously, counting off the days on her calendar, making sure she got lots of sleep and ate well, as you could never be too careful, and making sure Robert performed his duty during the times that mattered, she became pregnant. Mysteriously—alarmingly really—when she found out she had accomplished this well-planned goal, a knife-like terror shot through her and stayed, keeping her rigid with fear for nine long months.

Looking back, she now knew that it was the start of the ultimate contest, her most important competition. This was, of course, the cause of her anxiety. She wanted to do it better than her mother had. Indeed, she was fiercely determined to be a better mother, the best mother ever, in fact. She definitely planned on being better than the mothers in Central Park—she had lived briefly on the Upper West Side and would often have lunch on a park bench—who ignored their children while they chatted away with the other mothers. Or even worse, left them all day with exploited immigrants who could give two hoots about loving or caring for their charges. She envisioned herself thankful, never tired or angry, in a state of bliss resembling all those little babies at all those parties themselves. Mothers and babies, babies and mothers—innocent, happy and carefree. She would be patient, her baby's nose would never be dirty—the despair a dirty child pricked in her! How hard could it be to clean their little faces?!—and whenever her baby cried, she would comfort the baby with her arms and kisses. Often, she lay in bed at night, very awake, and thought about holding the baby that now grew in her belly. She'd rub her protruding stomach gently, and then, suddenly, the baby would move. For some reason, Lara found this very creepy. What was this thing? She knew it was going to be her baby, but now, moving around inside of her, it felt like a bony gas bubble. It felt like a crab, positively crustacean in its hardness. Occasionally she had nightmares about giving birth to a crab with human, baby features. The doctor would hand her this red-shelled creature. Panicked, she'd reach out for it, trying to hide her alarm. Then she'd wake up.

Robert would try to put his hand on her belly sometimes and ask to feel the baby. Lara would not let him. After dinner, after watching TV, they'd get into bed—she with her *New Yorker*, he with his *Artforum*—and he'd sidle up to her in a slimy way. His leg over her leg, his face on her neck. "Let me feel", he'd say softly, and it just disgusted her. In fact, Robert disgusted her in a way she'd never been disgusted with him before. Granted, men's bodies weren't very lovely, and so she'd always preferred to have the lights off. Then, in a dark room, occasionally, she liked the warmth of having sex with her husband. She liked the way she excited him. It made her feel important, or something. But now, now that she was pregnant, she could barely stand to look at him and the thought of him touching her body! Well, she just couldn't think about it. She'd kick his leg off of hers, arch her neck away from him and say, "Please! I'm trying to read." Eventually, he stopped trying to touch her or her belly, and, thank God, left her alone.

Despite the physically intense fear she carried during those long nine months, a few things seemed certain and reliable and comforted her during gestation. She would sit with her pint of ice cream in front of the TV, watching a sitcom, and think the comforting thought that inside her growing belly was a pretty little girl. A healthy, sweet-tempered girl who would grow up to shop with her, have her big milky, green eyes, talk about other people with her, and be kind and charming like her. So, after a grueling and humiliating labor ended in a Cesarean section, and the obstetrician held up an enormous, purpley and ugly little boy, she was shocked. A boy! Why, she didn't have any boy names picked out! His tiny ears looked like two miniature, crinkled vaginas, his eyes were hooded and dark, and his head was as pointy as a birthday hat. He looked nothing like her. He upset her so much that she cried and asked that he be taken to the nursery. It was like her dream in many ways, but she behaved worse in real life.

This was the first disappointment, and a big one. The shock of it lasted for weeks. This, coupled with recovering from the abdominal surgery, was no fun. In the beginning, all of her girlfriends came and cooed over the baby boy, but she could tell they thought he was ugly, too. Then, as the weeks went by and her energy returned to her, she began to see her baby in a different light. He had changed rapidly, thankfully, and so she felt some promise for a brighter future. His skin became smooth and cream colored, his pointy head rounded out, and he began to look around and make soft noises. She decided that his nose was the most perfectly shaped nose she had ever seen. Something stirred in her—was it love? Could it be love? Well, yes, that's what it could be! And why not? It was love and she was thrilled to feel it. This baby needed her! She was the absolute center of his life! She became proud and smitten and often could stare for long stretches at a time at his sleeping face.

But, weirdly, as her love for him grew in strength, so did a fresh, gripping panic and sadness. It dawned on her one night, as she paced around the never-ending cavern that was her loft (not Robert's, dammit, it was hers! Hers, hers, hers!) Holding the inconsolable, squalling infant, that he would cause her pain. That he was, in that very moment, causing her pain, and she hated him, deeply, hugely, and darkly so, for the psychic, emotional, and physical discomfort he was causing her. First the love and now the hate. Where did the love go, a love she'd only felt a few hours before? It was a distant, unbelievable memory. Alone, pacing back and forth in her chic loft, her husband undoubtedly snoring away in their king size bed with its feather mattress, the baby writhing and screaming and screaming and SCREAMING in her arms, there was no hiding that now all she felt for him was hate. Pure, liquid hate. She knew, at some point in the future this hatred of hers would be discernable to him—how can you hide hate?—and cause him pain. Rocking him back and forth in her arms, she became conscious of how tightly she gripped him—is that why he cried? Was she holding him so tightly it hurt?—And like a shot of vodka she imagined smashing his tiny, screaming head against the beautifully exposed brick wall. The thought simultaneously energized and relaxed her. The imagining of it—she saw her face angry, imagined the swinging of her arms, imagined his little face wide with horror and his tiny, helpless head thwacking against the wall—THWACK!—and blood spraying out everywhere—the picturing of this, scene by scene, cleared her head. She began breathing more steadily. She hadn't realized that she'd been holding her breath. Her arms went limp, and the baby, still crying—what was wrong with him?—nuzzled his head against her breast. She carried him into his room and put him down into his crib, still fucking crying, but with less energy now.

Feeling utterly spent, as if she'd run a marathon, she crawled into bed next to Robert. And yet, she couldn't sleep. She was haunted, frozen with the realization that her idea of blissful motherhood, blissful babyhood, had simply been that—an idea. In the other room, the baby had stopped crying. Lara shut her eyes, breathing deeply to try to make up for all that time she'd been holding her breath. The image of his little skull cracking open like a coconut, the sound of his screaming, crying head going thwack, oh, oh, the sound of it! She listened to the silence coming from his nursery. Should she check on him? Or would that wake him? Should she call the pediatrician tomorrow morning? She looked at the bedside clock and realized his crying jag had only lasted twenty minutes. It seemed so much longer than that! It had seemed like an hour, or more! Her lack of patience shocked her. Tears welled in her eyes; no, no, no—motherhood was not what she thought it would be. And no matter how hard she tried—and frankly, she didn't feel like trying very hard, she just wanted to sleep! To talk on the phone uninterrupted! Christ! To go to the bathroom uninterrupted!—She wouldn't be perfect. She would never be the perfect mother she'd imagined herself to be. All that time teaching pre-schoolers, all that time planning her wedding and trying to get pregnant and shopping for the nursery. But nor was her baby perfect, nor would he ever be. He wasn't already, in that he was a boy, for instance. She kept this newfound knowledge to herself, this realization of how flawed she and her son were, guarding it sacredly from her husband, from her mother—who called

Lara all the time now—and from all of her friends. It shamed her.

What was she going to do? Here she was, with a baby, the thing that she had always wanted, and she felt at loose ends. Hours could go by, and after much cooing and high-pitched baby talk, she had nothing to say to the baby. She'd get lost in thought, staring out a window or at a clothing catalogue, only to be shocked back to reality by his cry. And so she'd put him in the Peg Perego stroller, take him down the elevator, and stroll around. She shopped for groceries and bought herself new clothes. Robert, who worked long hours, told her to join a mothers' group. The idea repelled her for some reason. What if she didn't like the other mothers? And groveling for new friends didn't appeal to her. Her old friends from Smith who had bigger babies or children seemed so smug, saying, "It's hard, isn't it?" with a glint of satisfaction in their eyes. Or, "You'll never sleep again." She hated all the negativity. She loathed their condescension. But when she started cooking fish for dinner four nights a week, just so she could talk to the friendly guy at the fish store, she realized she needed company. That it was unhealthy for her to be spending so much time without adults. She'd begun mumbling and gesticulating to herself in the loft, walking around in circles while the baby napped in his crib. Had she gone crazy? Being alone with her baby was really being alone with her thoughts and this was no good.

At her next pediatrician appointment she furtively pulled a tab off of a flyer for a mothers' group in the neighborhood. She went home and immediately called Margaret, the name on the little piece of paper. An enthusiastic, young-seeming voice answered (she feared having to socialize with gray-haired, in vitro-fertilized mothers, of which there were plenty), and Lara nervously introduced herself, explaining how she got the number and how old her son was—he was three months old already! Margaret very cheerfully invited her to "join the group", which met every Friday morning, and everyone had to take turns buying bagels and hosting the other mothers. As Lara hung up, her heart filled with hope. Maybe, just maybe, this mothers' group would make her experience more pleasant. Even knowing that at the end of the week, she had somewhere to go, somewhere she was expected to be, made things better. Her week went by more quickly than ever—why did that feel good? Wasn't a child's infancy a time to be savored?—And Friday arrived, to Lara's alarming elation.

It took her a long time to get dressed. She was anxious *and* excited. Boots with heels or not? All black or not? She really hoped that Margaret didn't live in a dingy walk-up and wear sweatpants. That was the thing about Tribeca and the Village; some people had money, some didn't. Granted, most did, but one could never be certain. And Margaret's address wasn't a building that Lara knew offhand, so she couldn't be sure.

Shortly after college, Lara decided that it was OK she didn't like people who didn't have money. She found them tacky and depressing. She gave up trying to be liberal in that way of "money doesn't matter." It was an enormous relief. As it turned out, Margaret's building on Charles Street was a lovely doorman building, and Lara was delighted to ring the buzzer and be shown into an airy pre-war apartment with a large, well-furnished living room.

There were five other mothers there; everyone said hello and introduced themselves and their babies, "I'm Susan, this is Henry," and so forth. Only one of the mothers wore sweatpants, and they were nice ones, if such a thing can be said, and she made up for it by sporting a nice diamond bracelet. Margaret, who had opened the door and waved Lara into her apartment, was an attractive, smart-looking woman and immediately Lara hoped that they would be friends. She had long brown hair—Lara didn't like short hair on women—she wore no make-up and her diction was lovely. The conversation was lively and focused mainly on the babies, "She's just starting on rice cereal"; "He loves his bath"; "He doesn't sleep at all!", and occasionally digressed into complaints about absent, incompetent husbands, "He really is my first child, ha, ha, ha!" At some point during the chaotic small talk, Margaret turned to Lara and asked her, "Where are you from?"

"Greenwich." Lara replied, "And you?"

"Darien."

They smiled at each other, knowingly, Lara thought. A new friend! Robert was right. She needed this, needed other mothers in her life, and now, she realized, she had needed a new friend. Margaret's baby was a girl, a perfect little girl with Margaret's lovely dark features. Lara squelched her envy and looked straight into her new friend's fabulous, almond-shaped eyes, saying, "Where does your husband work?" Things went swimmingly from there. They had a lot in common. Lara left when everyone else did, hating to go, but not wanting to appear desperate—she wasn't going to be the last to leave! Walking home, pushing the Peg Perego with a sleeping baby in front of her, she felt better than she had in months.

At the beginning of the following week, On Monday, in fact, Lara decided to call Margaret and invite her over for lunch, just Margaret of course, not the entire mothers' group. She worried that this was a little on the aggressive side. Normally, she'd wait until the other woman invited her over. But she wanted the company and she felt quite confident that Margaret had liked her, too. They dressed alike, J.Crew with a little Prada thrown in, they both had Kate Spade diaper bags, neither of them breastfed, and there was the Darien/ Greenwich connection as well as both their husbands being graphic designers, although she had the feeling that her husband had more money than Robert, but Lara refused to dwell on that.

Lara put the baby in a vibrating plastic chair and propped him in front of the TV before picking up the phone. She was nervous, it was unlike her to be so forward, but she hid it well. Margaret was busy for lunch on Tuesday, but said, "What about Wednesday?", and so it was agreed. Lara was thrilled.

She didn't sleep very well on Tuesday night, because she was so excited. The next morning, she carefully rubbed gel on the bags under her eyes. She put on the new lipstick she had bought just for the occasion! It was pink, a reddish, slightly bold pink. She put the baby in the stroller and headed out to buy lunch. She planned on Balducci's or Dean & Deluca, and it was a nice day, so she'd take her time, stroll around and window shop. Lara ended up sitting on a park bench, sipping a latte and looking at *Vogue*. The baby had fallen asleep, and it was so early—still before 9:00—that there was no need to rush to get lunch. While she relaxed and looked at the magazine, Margaret and the woman with the diamond bracelet walked by together, both in stretchy, exercise pants and sneakers, with their babies in jogger-strollers. They were walking briskly, clearly on their way to the Hudson River to go running. They didn't stop, but waved and smiled. Margaret said, "See you at one o'clock!" Lara waved back stiffly, saying "See you!" As the two women passed her, Lara's hand remained frozen above in a hello/good-by salute, and she suddenly saw herself from outside of herself; stiff, her jaw clenched, a vibrant fear emanating from her very core, dark creases deepening around her mouth and eyes. She was alone—the baby did not count, no, in fact, it was his fault in some way, it was—she was bored, her lipstick was too bright, her clothes too expensive and her empty life glowed from every particle of her perfectly placed face powder. Never before had she felt so naked and so pathetic. She quickly got up and started hurrying toward Dean & Deluca.

The streets were crowded and her stroller seemed enormous and heavy. It was, in fact, enormous and heavy. It was the best goddamn stroller one could have. A man in a suit glared at her as she barreled down Spring Street. Her black clothes soaked up the April sun and she began to perspire from the exertion of pushing the stroller. The baby woke, startled by a bump on the sidewalk. He cried out and then, shocked by the rapid movement, his eyes wide open, immediately became quiet. She looked down at him in the stroller; his eyes wide, his lips drooly. Thwack, she thought. Thwack, thwack, thwack to you, she thought, as she looked down at him. When she turned her face back to the streets—the sun was so strong! When did it get this way? Where were her sunglasses?—another man in a suit looked at her strangely. Had she said thwack out loud? "Thwack!" She said it out loud purposefully this time, her head held high. "Thwack!" she said again, trying to feel in control. But she wasn't in control, really; she wasn't in control of so much of her life.

Having a baby, she realized, had been a failure of the imagination. She never could have imagined herself otherwise, other than as a pretty woman with a pretty baby. It never had dawned on her that having a baby wouldn't be fun, that when all those people said, "it's so much work", they meant it. She had never imagined such intense change in her life, such vulnerability. Lara loathed feeling vulnerable. Taking care of a baby had looked like so much fun; it had looked so *feminine*; so loving, so intimate and sweet. But the reality of changing diapers, of carrying the heavy —and getting heavier—little thing around, of waking up when *he* decided to wake up, all of this, every little bit of it, was a complete pain. It was drudgery. His smile was sweet, he did need her, but the novelty, or really, the power, of all those sweet things, wore off so quickly in face of the reality of what she did all day. Feed him, diaper him, dress him, try to comfort him, try to keep him clean, and always, always lug him around.

She reached Dean & Deluca. It was crowded. She had never been inside Dean & Deluca with her Peg Perego. Nasty looks came from everywhere. She felt huge and unwieldy and stood there, near the entrance. It was time to hire a nanny. She'd try and get an English or a French au pair, from a nice family. A young girl who'd pose no threat, have no authority. The aisles at

Dean & Deluca were so narrow, that it seemed clear the stroller wouldn't fit through them. What on earth would she serve for lunch? In which direction should she try to move? A tall, thin model glared at her, saying "Excuse me", as she pushed by. Lara felt fat and sweaty. Her hair hung damp and limp, clinging to her cheeks, making them itch a little. She was overcome with a strong feeling of contempt for the model that now stood behind her, in line at the register, buying a bottle of five dollar fruit juice. Fuck you, fuck you, fuck you! The thought of cursing the model out comforted her and reinforced the warm feeling coming over her; the only thing she'd ever been good at, really, really good at, (and she'd known this since she was a little girl, really, if she thought about it) was not liking other women. This was how she defined herself. This was how she made alliances. And it wasn't enough. No, it wasn't enough anymore. She'd have to learn something new.

Cheese, Lara thought. Good, French cheese and a loaf of bread. The baby started to cry. Someone had bumped the stroller and it startled him. Lara lifted him from the stroller, cooing gently in his ear and he quieted immediately. "Come now, sweet thing, come get some cheese with mummy, " Lara said, holding her little baby's face against her own, walking toward the ripe-smelling cheese counter, leaving the enormous, empty stroller at the front of the store where it would wait until she finished her shopping.

A WALK TO THE CEMETERY

What did it mean, to know inescapably that you married the wrong person? That you made a terrible mistake? Perhaps for some, it meant organizing a divorce. But Greta wasn't so sure. If for no other reason, she wouldn't want to give her mother-in-law the satisfaction. And yet, she'd known since they bought the house. Perhaps she'd known since 9/11. It wasn't something she talked to anyone about. It wasn't something that she even thought in solid sentence formation; it wasn't as if she sat around thinking, *I've married the wrong person.* And yet the knowledge was there inside of her, choking her lungs and burning her stomach, furrowing her brow with concerns for the children, the houses. She'd married the wrong man.

It wasn't because they didn't have sex, although they hadn't had sex in two years. At first, Greta stopped fucking him for some inane, but insanely persistent reason; he wouldn't empty the garbage, he wouldn't put his dirty socks and underwear in the laundry basket, he always forgot to ask the kids to brush their teeth if—God forbid! —she asked him to put the kids to bed. But then, she just kept not fucking him. To see what he'd do, to see what he'd say. And he did nothing. And he never said anything. And it had been two years. No, it wasn't for any concrete reason. It was because she'd married him under the wrong assumption—she'd married him because he enjoyed her love so much, that she thought he'd actually loved her back. And she was wrong about that.

"I'm taking David for a walk," Greta declared tensely. The rain had been making her tense. And aggravating her stomach problems. Doctor after doctor had little help for her. She quit drinking coffee. She quit drinking wine for awhile, but started again. It wasn't good for her stomach problems, but she couldn't live without it.

David was her older boy, her first-grader. He was often tense too, and Greta blamed herself, most likely rightly so. As the oldest, he seemed to absorb whatever emotional climate was floating around. This usually meant repressed rage, irritation, sourness. Greta would look at him and see her own miserable state. Sometimes it was too much; she'd go and read a magazine. Other times, she'd try to have "alone time" with him, give him some special attention, hoping to make amends, to make things better.

It was not easy walking in the country, or at least Greta didn't find it so. This was one of the many disappointments with the house. They were here for fresh, clean air, and yet they spent an inordinate amount of time indoors, even if it wasn't raining, although it had been raining forever at this point. Walking along the side of the road meant constantly listening and looking for cars and the vast, beastly trucks which everyone seemed to drive, and she often had to stumble off the road, which sometimes meant into a rather deep ditch filled with water. Rubber boots helped a bit, but a big truck blowing by was a big truck blowing by, regardless of footwear. And then there were the dogs: vicious, miserable things that no one paid any attention to, sometimes chained up, but often not. They were, without a doubt, the real danger. She knew she should start seriously gardening--that would keep her outside. But it was hard when they were only there on weekends, and then not even every weekend. She had tried planting some things. They all mostly dried up and died.

"Why can't I come with you, mommy?" William said. He looked sad. Four-year-olds looked sad so easily. They didn't know how to hide their true emotions yet.

"David and I need a little alone time, sweetie. We'll be right back." She blew him a kiss and they started out.

The air was cool. She looked to make sure David was wearing a jacket: he was—a good, rainproof parka. She herself had on an Austrian boiled wool jacket her mother had given her; her mother was Austrian, and although Greta was raised in the Midwest, her mother had returned to Austria after the children were grown. Greta owned at least ten of these jackets. They were not particularly good in damp weather. They got smelly and the heaviness wasn't really appropriate, either.

Immediately, David lagged behind. He scuffed his boots on the road, looking down. The walk took only fifteen minutes and there was no hurry, but still. Why did he have to be so sullen? So difficult? Their house was on River Road, which curved around a cemetery and then let onto Sherman Creek Road, which led to the Delaware. They would be passing five or six houses along the way, two with dogs. The first house, their neighbor's, was one with a dog. But Greta knew this dog, Sugar, a sandy-colored Chow. Greta wasn't afraid of him, not really, although he was never chained and barked furiously. As they approached the house, she began walking a little faster, with more purpose. Fuck him, she thought about David. I won't let him watch his fucking video if he's going to be so gloomy and unenthusiastic. Then Sugar came out of the house, but not very far. She commenced barking. Greta felt brave and determined and she walked even more quickly.

"Hey, wait up," David said, and ran to catch up with her. David didn't seem afraid of Sugar, but there was something about being barked at; it just made one hurry.

"You could try not lolling behind with your face in your collar," she snapped. "This is supposed to be a nice time together."

"It wasn't my idea." He said. He looked hurt, guilty.

"I know it wasn't your idea," she hollered, even though Sugar had gone inside and there was no barking to try and be heard over. Indeed, they'd passed the neighbor's house. They were coming upon the cemetery now. She'd ruined it, again. Like always. Lost her temper again. They walked quietly for a moment and Greta's chest closed up like a fist. She tried to breathe deeply, but she could only manage shallow, quick breaths. Her asthma flaring. She was so impatient. She always lost it, always. It killed her. The one thing she wanted to do was be loving to her sons. She could do it sometimes, be loving, but only fleetingly.

They heard a vehicle approaching. She grabbed David's arm a bit too roughly and pulled him off the side of the road with her. A car drove by, much faster than it should. After they passed, Greta paused for a moment. Something made her think of a cheap perfume she wore in high school. It was the clovers by the side of the road. Purple, knotted little things, weeds really, but they filled the air with such sweetness, even on this rainy, cold day. Barking dogs, tense words with one's children, a car barreling down the road; and yet, this gift of perfume. She began walking slowly, consciously trying to keep David near her. He was still looking down, still dragging his feet noisily. He's just a boy, thought Greta. He's just a seven-year-old boy.

When they were thinking of buying the house, the cemetery appealed to Greta. It was on a gentle hill, a small cemetery, with some very old headstones and, of course, some new ones. Greta had thought it would be a wonderful place to be buried. It wasn't something she thought about often, dying, and Richard and she hadn't even made out wills yet.

It began to rain a little.

"Hey, Mom. It's starting to rain. Can we go back?"

He was using his nice voice. He looked chastened. God, she loved her son so much. But so often she looked at him and saw her own failures. And it killed her.

"Let's at least walk up to the cemetery," she said. " And sit for a minute."

David scowled and started to walk quickly ahead of her.

When David had been an infant, she and Richard had fought viciously. He was never home before nine o'clock—that had started during her pregnancy. When he was home, he poked around the refrigerator, looking for food. Or he sat on the couch, farting and reading the paper, with the TV on. She thought she was going to go mad. He was no help. At all. He was the opposite of help. He brought more work to a home she could barely handle. They had no money then—she had no babysitter, no household help at all. And her husband just wanted to be fed and have his underwear picked up off the floor. And so, one Friday night when he returned home around ten and went straight for the refrigerator she followed him into the kitchen.

"I want you to move out."

"Excuse me?" He said, but he didn't turn his head, and he didn't close the refrigerator.

"I want you to move out. You come home late every night. You don't help with the baby. You are useless. Out. I want you out of here." Her voice was shaking. Her whole body was shaking.

He closed the fridge. "Fuck you. You move out. I pay the rent here. You fucking move out."

And so she picked up a knife. A large carving knife. She hadn't planned on picking up the knife, but, well, they were in the kitchen and there was the knife. As if it were meant to be. She had planned on asking him to leave. But she hadn't planned on picking up the knife. But something took over. She lost it. "GET THE FUCK OUT OF HERE NOW OR I'M GOING TO KILL MYSELF! GET OUT! GET OUT!" She held the knife tightly against her neck and walked toward him. And he went. He left. She put the knife back on the magnetic knife rack her father had given her. There was some blood on her blouse. Not much. She'd cut herself slightly. He stayed away for two nights, and then when he returned—knocking on the door to be let in because Greta had the chain up—he was apologetic and sheepish. He said he'd try to be home at a more reasonable hour. He said he'd try to be helpful. She felt forgiving, which, looking back now, was the biggest mistake. Because the minute she forgave him anything, he forgot there was anything that she was ever angry about. Richard was Richard, and he wasn't one to worry about things, particularly not things like his marriage.

Greta had a slight raised line of a scab on her neck for a week or so after the knife incident. She fingered its rough, bumpy edges lovingly, particularly at night. It was a soothing, calming thing, putting her to sleep like a strong scotch would have. She was sad when the scab went away, leaving no scar. For weeks afterward, she'd finger where it had been, forlornly. Her fingers would go to her neck at night, full of hope, and there was nothing there. Then she stopped, of course. She was, for the most part, highly adaptable, like most human beings.

Looking back, the knife incident was clearly a high point in their marriage. It was a rare moment when Richard listened to her. But it was too much work. She couldn't pull a knife on herself every time she wanted Richard to listen to her. It just wasn't worth it.

They reached the cemetery. A small, sloping hill full of graves, headstones, both old and new. There were three stone steps that led to a sort of pathway that went down the middle of the graveyard and a sign: Hale Eddy Cemetery. The rain was more of a mist now, but it was unpleasant. David tramped ahead until midway, where he sat on a big, crumbling stump. He had his hands shoved angrily in his pockets. "Now can we go?" he spat at her.

This walk was a disaster. She could barely breathe and she didn't have her inhaler on her.

Her son was furious at her. They were wet and uncomfortable and they still had another dog to navigate before they got to the river. Greta felt ashamed of her bad idea. She went and sat down next to her son.

She had once loved him so profoundly; when he was two, three, four. He had been adorable, eager to please, affectionate. And what about five and six? She must have loved him then, too, but she remembered those years less, because that was when William was getting more demanding. They must have been transition years in some way, a transition to this seven-year-old, to this defiant, sullen being. He was so annoyed with her, so angry with her. He was tall and skinny and beginning to show signs of the awkward pre-adolescent he would soon be. This, at seven. Who knew? She still loved him, but it was with great pain and confusion. What had happened to her little boy? He had turned into this medium-sized boy, with a will of his own. She feared coming down too hard on him, although God knows she did anyway, but it seemed to backfire. His disrespect for her just grew in those instances. How to win him back? Buying him Legos or computer games didn't work. They were immediately taken for granted. What could she do?

She remembered then, when he was a baby, a tiny, screaming, red-faced infant. Then, too, she had felt much pain—the pain of sleep deprivation, the pain of no freedom, the pain of being utterly alone with this infant. And that pain had passed. He had grown into a joyful, brilliant toddler. And this would pass, too. He would turn eight and then nine, and so on, and he would change. And she would just suffer or enjoy him, depending. This time, too, would pass. But one thing seemed certain—she was no longer the source of his joy, and she never would be again, not in the same way she once was. He needed her, yes, and perhaps he loved her, although she doubted this sometimes. He wanted things from her—his meals, toys, help with his homework—but what went on inside his heart? His mind? She once felt she knew everything about him, and now he was such a mystery. Sitting there next to him in the rain, it struck her that William was the one who wanted her now, not David. That maybe, like weaning him from the breast, it was time to let go. That all of her energy and effort were being poured into the wrong person, into her son who desperately needed his space. And back at home was a cuddly toddler, who probably missed her even in these few minutes that she'd been gone.

Right next to the stump where they sat was a fresh grave. She hadn't noticed it when they first sat down. But there it was, a mound of brown dirt turning dark from the rain, smelling fresh and earthy. Flowers and ribbons scattered around it.

"Look, David, a fresh grave."

David looked at it and his face opened up a bit. His lips were blue from the cold. He looked away. And who could blame him? Greta stared. She imagined the body underneath, lying on white satin inside of the coffin. The features sunk deeply into the skin, the cavities in our bodies— the eyes, the mouth, the nostrils—all sucking in the rest of us. The black hole of death.

Greta had watched her father die in her early twenties. Sitting next to his bed, listening to the rough, desperate pulls of breath. He'd opened his eyes that night, and seen her. The nurse swabbed petroleum jelly on his lips. His eyes looked wild. He tried to speak, but only managed a grunt. Nonetheless, it seemed he was trying to comfort her. He was dead the next morning. A corpse. A pale, little husk of life. After that, Greta had spent months in therapy, months on anti-depressants, and then she discovered yoga. She stopped taking drugs and started doing a lot of yoga. During that time, she spent two weeks at an ashram upstate. It was run by westerners primarily, but it was a strict Hindu ashram. She did four hours of yoga every day, tried to meditate, and even participated in chanting and listened to the talks given after every satsang. At the end of the two weeks, she felt she'd been gone for years. She'd also managed to make no friends during her stay. It was then that she realized she was a cold person. That rarely did she trust someone, and then, perhaps all too completely. She lacked balance; the very thing yoga was trying to give her. She also realized that God was about death. That worshipping God was about dealing with death. She hadn't known that, surely, when she started doing yoga, and she didn't know it really until after she left the ashram. But then she knew, afterward. To believe in God is to soothe the fear of our death. And when she realized that, she wondered, why worry about death when you are twenty-five? Or forty? Why practice staying still, why meditate, when in old age, you will be stilled, and then, you will die? Why not wait until you can't help it? Why force a young body, so full of movement and life and desire, to be still? To not desire?

In the graveyard that day with her son, she thought, because we don't know when it will come.

"Someone recently got buried there." She said.

"Yeah, I figured that. Creepy. Mom, can we go?"

"Yeah, we can go."

"Back to the house?"

"Yes." She said, "Did you know that elephants bury their dead?"

"Huh?"

"Elephants take their sick and dying to the same spot. They have graveyards, just like humans. Scientists have found great big piles of elephant bones."

Now David looked a bit curious. "Do they carry them? Do they carry them with their trunks?"

"I don't know. Good question. But I think they love each other. I think how we treat our dead is an act of love. And I think they are the only animals who do that, who have graveyards. I'm not sure. Probably whales do too, somewhere deep in the oceans." Greta looked around at the gray headstones. It was the most we could do for the dead. Love as well as the elephants do. We would be doing well if we could do as well as those magnificent beasts. And for the living?

"Mom, it's really raining. Let's go."

He was right, it was really raining. This tall child, this product of her love for Richard. Seven years ago seemed a lifetime. The very idea that she had loved Richard passionately seemed strange and distant, like a movie she'd seen years ago, not even like a part of her own life. She was not the same person she was then, although most people, from just looking at her, probably thought she hadn't changed at all. She hadn't gained much weight, she kept her hair blonde by highlighting it. But inside, inside, despite her children, despite all her luck and ease in life, inside, she felt her heart had turned black. Every year, and really, every day of every year, of all the years of her marriage to Richard, she became, slowly, a smaller person—less capable of joy, of generosity. She missed being generous the most. She had had an enormous capacity to give. No longer. Now, everything was a calculation, everything was bartered. Meanwhile, Richard had turned into a decent, successful man after spending most of his twenties being a bratty, snotty, spoiled boy. She had forced him to grow up, hold down a job, and be kind to his children—none of which he would have accomplished without her. He had become better with the years, he had fed off the marriage, and she had become not only worse, but unrecognizable. She had become sour and ugly (despite looking the same on the outside, her insides showed through, they did) and (rightly so) suspicious. And now, she was sickly to boot. She had become, in other words, someone to be avoided.

In a Graham Greene novel she'd read years ago, when she still thought herself capable of happiness, she'd come across some interesting lines that had stuck with her, haunting her. At the time that she read the novel, she still thought if she did and said the right things—if she tried to be good, and honest, and if she were giving and loving—happiness would come. The book had shocked her. In it, a priest harshly condemns a woman, saying, "And do you think God's likely to be more bitter than a woman?" The words had hurt her at the time, but they came to her now, almost as a salve, and very much as the truth. There had been that friend of hers in college, a boy she thought she loved and who flirted with her but who would not date her, because she wasn't Jewish. He had told her once, mischievously, that every morning he prayed, "Thank you God, for not making me a woman." Again, she'd been appalled at the time, but now it seemed an answer. It wasn't that women had no souls, but she'd almost never met a woman who wasn't grasping desperately to her resentments.

And yet, there had been times she'd wanted to shout at Richard, "You have no love to give! You have no love to give!", but not with bitterness, not with resentment. She wanted to shout this in relief and joy, with the knowledge she had been looking for something that didn't exist. She'd been chasing ghosts. The love she needed wasn't from Richard, no. He had none. (And often, she felt sorry for him, she felt the need to protect him from his own, empty self.) She'd been looking in the wrong place.

"Let's go," she said and stood up. David jumped up and ran ahead, down to the road. The mist was so strong, she couldn't see the hills. They walked in silence, until they came to their neighbor's house, where Sugar emerged from the gray fog and commenced barking. She barked furiously, but stayed put, a good way away from them.

"You go back without me," She wheezed. "I'm going to the river. You go back."

David's face crumbled. For a moment, she was reminded of him as a toddler; a needy, sensitive, tow-haired little baby boy. "I can't go back alone." he protested.

"Yes you can," Greta said. It was true. Boys his age who lived around here often walked around alone or with friends for short distances. She saw them all the time, enthralled by the freedom the country gave young kids. Hell, once she met an eight-year-old out on their property, dressed in camouflage and shooting at squirrels with a real gun.

"This is our next door neighbor's house. It'll take you two minutes or so to get onto our property, onto our yard."

"Mom!"

"Go. I'm going. You'll be fine." And she turned her back on him (although she could hear him, hear him running down the road in his rubber boots), and she began walking back toward the cemetery and beyond, to face more nasty dogs, more rain, and then, finally, the river, the brown, dirt-filled, moving body of water, that was one of the reasons they were here.

SUPERSTITION

He married his wife because she was rich. Eight years ago now, he had reconciled himself with her less desirable features—her enormous ass, her skinny shoulders and small breasts, her horsey, thick ankles, her grating voice that resembled the yapping of a Shih Tzu dog—and focused on her charms. She had gleaming, long wheat-colored hair, thick and lustrous and horsey as well. Often while fucking her from behind, which was his favorite way to fuck her, he grabbed her mane and tugged at it to make her say, "Ow, ow, ow". Other times he bent over her long, white spine and pressed his face into the shockingly beautiful hair, inhaling the sweet shampoo smell of apricots. She had a lovely mouth. Her lips were perfectly pink, not grossly voluptuous and not thin, either. He had never once seen a pimple on her face. She drank very little and didn't smoke or sunbathe and her skin was like moist ivory, like a little girl's skin, even now, in her mid-thirties. In other words, she had some good features.

And, primarily, she was stinking, filthy rich. A Park Avenue girl to the core—Brearley, Andover, Barnard, summers in a ridiculously huge, seven bedroom house in Southampton—this was Cricket's life. The life that he and his divorced, former model of a mother, who ended up working in publishing, watched happen around them with an envy that never once let them breathe a full breath one minute of their Second Avenue, cat urine-smelling, four story walk-up living, lives. If he thought about his meeting Cricket at a party, then their dating and socializing in New York, now so long ago—ten years ago! An entire decade ago!—he would still swell with pride. He'd bagged her. Nailed her. He'd got her under his thumb with the brute luck of his tall, underwear model (he had a huge dick) handsomeness, combined with his evenness—he wasn't spoiled enough to have a drug problem and lose jobs constantly like many of her wealthy friends—and his dogged persistence. Her parents fussed over her older, prettier sister, who married well, and their favorite child, their son, who also married well, and so they didn't protest too much when Cricket announced that she was marrying him. George Severs married a Park Avenue girl. The joy and pride it brought his mother was worth anything. His soul, if he had one, his happiness, if he knew what that meant. It was as if all the terrible things that had happened to his mother—losing her looks as she got older, her husband leaving her for his secretary (when George was only two years old) and having four kids with her, her subsequent degrading job and small, cheerless apartment—none of these things mattered anymore. His marriage erased her bitterness; he had redeemed her.

And so, when she died of breast cancer last year, George had almost not been sad. She had died so happy. He, *he*, George Severs, the average student, the son who hadn't gotten into any of his top choice colleges, not Columbia, not Berkeley, not Amherst, finally attending Connecticut College (which wasn't so bad), he had, finally, made his mother deeply and truly happy. She died quietly and rather quickly. Who knows if the doctors could have done more? She had been unreliable about getting check-ups and so was diagnosed pretty late in the game.

A year had passed now since her death. A year! And now, after work sometimes, George found himself going not straight home to their townhouse on Ninety-Fourth Street between Madison and Fifth, which Cricket's dad had paid for half of as a wedding present, but rather to his old block. He got off the train two stops early and walked east of Lexington, to the corner of Second and Seventy-First, to the apartment building where she had lived until she died in the hospital, the apartment building where he grew up. A tall, respectable-looking building, pre-war, yes, but with an indisputable tenement-y vibe to it. He could see apartment 4F's windows from where he sat in the Greek diner across the street. Cricket had helped him get rid of the worn, not really antique, just old, furniture. She called the pound that collected the two cats. George kept one trunk, full of curling snapshots; it collected dust in the basement of their townhouse. His mother had rented the apartment and so Cricket called a broker and it was rented out to someone else immediately.

George sat by the window in the diner, trying not to be recognized, and watched people come home from work, watched them pull out their keys, their heads bowed as they let themselves into the building. After an hour or two of this, he walked home quickly, his massive frame and large stride inadvertently forcing people off to the edges of the sidewalk. He didn't notice this happening. He walked up Second all the way to Ninety-Fourth. Years ago, he never would have walked up Second. Why do that? Why not cross over and look at the nice shops on Madison, or walk up the wide expanse of Park? But here he was, trudging up an undesirable avenue. And while he walked home, certain alarming, strange thoughts circled inside his brain—what's so wrong with Second Avenue? What was so awful about their lives, his and his mother's? The people letting themselves into his old building—they didn't seem any less happy or less *important* than the people on his new block. They didn't seem *lesser* at all.

When he arrived home, these crazy thoughts were gone. Thankfully. Cricket sat in the living room drinking a glass of Chardonnay, classical music playing, a thick, Italian fashion magazine in her lap. She did not look up as he noisily entered their house. Their three-year-old son, Charlie, was already in bed. George was grateful Charlie was asleep. Charlie had his mother's thick, wheat-colored hair, but otherwise, looked exactly like George and had since the day he was born. Big, blue eyes set wide in a rectangular shaped face. A prominent forehead. Sometimes, while reading to him at night, or helping him out of his pajamas on Saturday morning, George felt like he was physically up against a tiny, pre-formed blossom of himself, and that every little thing he did mattered more than any one human could possibly withstand. His hands trembling, he felt that the slightest, awkward maneuver would destroy his little clone and possibly destroy himself as well. It was all very confusing. In an effort to pull up Charlie's pajamas, occasionally George's finger pressed against his miniature bottom. This filled George with disgust and fear and he'd pull his hand back from his son's flesh, forcing the elastic to snap against the poor boy. Even the acrid smell of his post-work, post-subway ride armpits as they sat side by side on the couch, father and son, reading *Goodnight Moon*, seemed poisonous and ruinous. The pressure! George, on numerous occasions, broke into an icy sweat and called desperately, in a deep, curt voice, for Cricket's help. She would come in and relieve him of his duty, annoyed yet understanding, thinking George, like many husbands, didn't have the patience to deal with children.

Coming home late after his Second Avenue visits, dinner waited on the marble kitchen counter for George, in the form of a plate neatly displayed with some kind of meat, a vegetable, and a starch. He'd put the plate in the microwave and press reheat. The food was often from a gourmet takeout, and just as often cooked by Cricket. She took cooking classes, and her dinners were indistinguishable from the takeout places she frequented. He used to say to her, "This is great! This tastes like it came from Antoine's!" thinking this was a nice thing to say. For a long time, Cricket said, "Thanks!" and smiled. Then, once, suddenly, she said, in the most Shih Tzu-yapping, high register she could achieve, "I find it insulting that the food I fucking slaved over to make for you, you think I picked up at the corner." His fork stopped midway to his mouth. She looked straight at him, holding his gaze with the glee of triumph. He thought, you lying, trap-setting, fake-as-shit cunt. And yet he said nothing and proceeded to finish shoveling the raspberry chicken into his mouth. She snapped herself up and went for the kitchen and he listened to her heels click-clacking smartly on the Mexican tiles as she started to clean up. Clack, clack went her shoes, and then the sound of water pouring forcefully into the sink. For a while then, he thought about how her smiles and thanks had not been genuine. They had seemed genuine to George. His appreciation, while perhaps overly earnest, had been real. He felt stupid, naive. He thought he was making her happy, in return for her making him happy. He had been wrong. And yet, life continued normally, of course. Cricket smiled often, slept well, rose early, and chatted eagerly to George about other families with whom they socialized. But George never believed her as he had before the incident. He stopped believing anything she said, really, unless it was a straightforward, nasty comment, of which, despite her generally upbeat nature, there were plenty. It dawned on him that she probably had no genuine feelings of the positive variety. From then on, he assumed that when she smiled, which she did quite often, that she didn't mean it. He knew that lurking behind her spunky appearance was an angry, calculating bitch.

And yet the thought of actually leaving Cricket filled him with despair. It reminded him of the drunks he met while tending bar in New London. While in college, he worked at a divey sort of place to make money for books and living expenses. It was populated by some Conn College students, but also by "townies" as the residents of New London were known to the students. One night, Chris, a townie, a cab driver who often drove visiting parents to their children's dorm rooms, a fifty-year-old alcoholic and cocaine addict, tried to wipe some sweat off of his face and his skin rubbed off and blood starting coming out and it didn't stop. George called an ambulance. During the next few weeks, the other townie regulars would come in and tell George what had happened. Chris had almost died. His liver had stopped working. But after three months in detox, Chris returned to the bar, a different Chris in many ways, but the same Chris in a unique, astonishing aspect. He was thirty pounds thinner, he had lost his pallor, and he drank club sodas, no lemon, and very little ice, instead of vodka. He no longer was the biggest, loudest, most obnoxious man in the bar. In his place the new Chris sat, a meek, sad, bitter man, holding forth on the same subject matters as always— baseball, the best way to get somewhere in the town, the nature of the spoiled college kids and their snobby parents. He had been a horrible drunk. But a jolly, horrible drunk. Boisterous, cheery, red-faced. Now, without alcohol, everything about him that had once seemed stupid and obnoxious now seemed terribly sad and fearful. He hadn't really changed, he would never really change. He just wasn't drunk anymore. George could barely look at him.

George knew if he left Cricket, he would probably be free of something awful, but he would still be George Severs, and he was pretty sure he didn't want to discover what that was.

There *were* nice things about Cricket that confused him. She overpaid her maid and nanny, because she truly felt they deserved to be paid well. Once, the nanny gave Cricket a bright pink T-shirt from the Gap for Christmas. It was sinfully cheap looking but Cricket wore it all the time anyway, without complaining. She was polite to waiters. She loved her son and took wonderful care of him. (And yet she refused to have more children, which was fine with George.) She planned great vacations twice a year for the family. She never, ever complained about how much time he spent at work—he was an investment banker—nor how little money he made. His marriage was, by all means, a success. For their eight year anniversary, they flew to Venice for a long weekend without Charlie. It was nice. He read all of *Smart Money, Fortune, Fast Company* and part of a biography about David Geffen. She read the ever-present thick fashion magazines and shopped. She shipped some furniture back to New York. They drank a lot of wine and at night, finished their dinners with grappas.

That had been months ago. It was fall now. After their Venice trip, Cricket and Charlie summered in Southampton and so he had only seen them on the weekends then, when he went out to her family home. It was during the summer, while they were gone, that he had started to make his trips to Second Avenue. No one and no dinner waited at home for him, he had reasoned. And so he ate at the diner by himself, at the same booth, with great regularity, looking wistfully and with great confusion at his former building. Summer was over now. He assumed he would stop going once Cricket and Charlie returned, but that had not happened. Now, instead of just feeling bizarre and overwhelmed by his compulsive after-work detours, he also felt ashamed, as if he were hiding something, which, in fact, he was, when he returned to their house.

Of course, Cricket never asked him why he was always late, why every night he now came home at least an hour later than he used to come home. That would have been straightforward, and Cricket, as he had discovered, was not straightforward. And so, whereas once he would have come home amid the hectic nighttime ritual of putting Charlie to bed, and whereas once Cricket and he would have suppered together after Charlie lay asleep, passing little bits of gossip and family planning back and forth across the table, now he returned late, and ate his microwaved plate of food standing up in the kitchen, while his wife sat in the living room with her wine and magazine and soothing Mozart. After he wolfed down his dinner, he'd come into the living room, maybe read the paper. They'd exchange some pleasantries, but because of his shame, or because of his lateness, or because something inexplicable had changed, a former intimacy inherent to their conversation was lost. George felt relief in this new, more distant interaction with his wife. He preferred sitting across the wide expanse of their living room from her, as opposed to the close proximity they once shared sitting at the corner of their mahogany dinner table, their elbows nearly grazing, her narrow brown eyes an arm's length away. Later, in bed, in the darkness, he had fewer troubles with Cricket. They fucked twice a month like clockwork, but in the dark like that, doing what they'd always done—no surprises for either of them—he didn't feel intimate. He didn't feel threatened or out of control. He didn't fear that he wanted to backhand his wife, because the violence he acted out on her with his dick sufficed.

It wasn't until the middle of November that Mrs. Ferguson approached George at the diner. He was at his booth drinking coffee, his briefcase lying on the table in front of him. "George, is that you?" She lurched toward his table, bags in hand, her mouth a smear of orangey lipstick. "I thought that might be you!"

"Mrs. Ferguson!" George stood and air kissed her cheek. His mother had been good, neighborly friends with this old busybody. And when his mother became sick, it was true that Mrs. Ferguson had been helpful and kind and ran errands for her and even brought her homemade casseroles and lasagnas regularly. After she died, George had to return a number of baking pans to Mrs. Ferguson. And when they were overseeing the removal of the furniture, Mrs. Ferguson came out into the hallway, tears in her eyes, blabbering on about how wonderful George's mother had been. He remembered how he awkwardly asked her if there was anything she wanted from the apartment. He explained that he and Cricket didn't need any furniture, and beyond a few keepsakes, everything else was going to be given away. Would she like a chair, an end table? Her tears quickly dried up as she picked through an assortment of furniture, choosing a rather newly-upholstered wingback chair. His mother had loved that chair. The movers took it to her apartment and he walked in with them momentarily. There really was not enough space for the chair, but they managed to shove it into her living room somehow.

"Why, I said to myself, could that be George Severs? I ran out to the CVS to get some toilet paper..."

"How are you?" George boomed at her, shaking her hands too aggressively. "How's the chair?"

"The chair?" Mrs. Ferguson seemed confused. "Oh yes, the chair is fine."

"Well, I'm just finishing some coffee, just had a meeting here with a junior associate, it's a late night, and I better be on my way." He shook her hands again. "Great seeing you."

"You know, it's funny,' Mrs. Ferguson said, hoisting a bag full of toilet paper on her hip, "but as I walked by on my way to CVS, I thought, who's that man, looking out the window? Why, he looks so familiar. And the whole time I was in CVS I was thinking that maybe it was you. And, I have worried about you, George. I know how you loved your mother. I didn't see your associate, and I was thinking maybe..."

"Ah, yes, he left and I'm just trying to get the energy to get going! It's a little cold out there, you know!" George was nearly yelling. "Great seeing you!" He went for the door after he leaned in for another air kiss, this time managing to make a loud smacking noise into the old woman's ear. He felt her startle, but he kept going, out the door, into the not-so-cold November night, and because he was disoriented from running into Mrs. Ferguson, he started walking down Second Avenue instead of up. After a block or so, when he regained his equilibrium, he decided to just keep walking downtown. He stopped into a bar and drank a quick shot of whiskey. Heat poured into his face. Uneasy, he walked out to Second again and thought what the heck? Why not go all the way to the Village? Why not take a cab? When was the last time he was downtown, unless, of course, he was on Wall Street? During college, he and some of his buddies over the holiday breaks would meet at clubs downtown and check out all the weird, arty chicks. And during boarding school, he and his buddies lived for downtown. Nobody carded them at the bars or delis, and often they'd buy a six pack of beer each and go "stooping". This involved sitting on other people's stoops near Washington Square Park, each drinking their six beers and smoking grass bought from some dealer in the park. Drunk and high and excited to be alive, with great curiosity, they watched gay men and NYU students walk by, until a tenant or owner on whose steps they were stooping asked them to leave. But sometimes, rather than being asked to leave, a resident would sit and drink with them. This was always very exciting.

The cab dropped him off at the entrance to the park. He walked through it and was amazed to see professional men and women taking their dogs out or holding the hands of their children. Where were the dealers? The club kids? Eventually, near the west entrance of the park, he saw some Rastas selling weed. He bought a tiny little bag of what seemed to be a sticky bud of pot and realized he'd have to go and buy a pipe to smoke it in. He left the park and walked around, not really knowing where he was going, everything seeming familiar and yet he had no idea where he was. Waverly? MacDougal? He found a brightly lit head shop, with vibrators, pipes, and bongs gleaming vulgarly in the window. He purchased a tiny brown pipe and some screens.

George returned to the park. The night was very mild, not cold at all, not moist or dry, but perfectly balanced, only the smallest breeze dropping leaves lazily to the ground. To sit on a park bench, the air sweet and good, and a real bud of pot in hand! Nostalgia coursed through him, leaving him soft and weak. He smoked. One Thanksgiving break, eagerly fleeing Kent for the week, he'd brought home with him a boy from Utah, who couldn't afford to fly home for the holiday. His name was Lance Summa, a scholarship boy, who, although very smart, was somewhat of a troublemaker and barely made it through Kent without getting booted out. He had asked George if he could come home with him and George had said yes because George wasn't very good at saying no. George's mother didn't mind so much. She had felt sorry for Lance when George had explained his situation.

Although Lance was clearly an outsider at Kent, he was cool too, in a dark, mysterious way. He listened to Black Sabbath and Led Zeppelin instead of The Talking Heads and The Grateful Dead. Skinny and high-strung, but often generous, Lance was known to share his homework, albeit only after insulting the intelligence of the borrower. He could do a barrel of drugs and still talk his way eloquently through Vespers and dinner. No one could figure him out, but he undoubtedly impressed his classmates. When the boys, carrying duffel bags full of laundry over their shoulders, walked up the stairs and into the apartment, George's mother was still at work. It was early evening on a Friday night. The traffic could be heard loudly, even though they were four stories up. George realized Lance was the first Kent boy who'd been in his apartment. Lance looked around, but didn't reveal any feelings whatsoever. "Where do we crash?" he asked, and George saw that he didn't think badly of where George lived, because he didn't know well enough to think anything at all.

The first few nights they hung out with other Kent boys, in Park Avenue apartments, getting drunk on the booze of parents who'd left the kids in New York while they went to their homes in the Caribbean. That had been lots of fun. But on the night before Thanksgiving, with nothing to do, they took a cab downtown and bought pot and got stoned in the park. Then they purchased six packs and found a nice stoop to sit on. It was a night like tonight, a perfect night for sitting on a stoop. The owner of the brownstone came out and sat with them. They shared their beer with him and he had more pot, which he rolled expertly into joints and passed around. He was a gay man, in his early forties maybe, with delicately styled blond hair.

Lance went inside with the man. George was really fucked up—high, drunk and profoundly happy to be so. When Lance came back out, he was reeling. "Oh, man, Mr. Fagboy has some serious shit in there!" Snorting and breathing weirdly, Lance continued, "Coke, rush, the works! It's your turn, Big-Dick. Don't be superstitious, it doesn't mean anything and he's not gonna hurt you. He's gonna love you." George went inside. Superstitious? What did Lance mean? The walls were painted dark green. On the zebra-print couch sat the man, with a mirror full of pristine, cut lines of cocaine. "Your friend told me all about you," he said, smiling shyly.

It was George's first blow job in his life, and remained the best.

The next morning, George's mother, stepping over the sleeping Lance, sat next to her only son on his childhood twin size bed, a bed still covered with sheets printed with rockets and astronauts, and stroked his back with two fingers, just how he had liked it as a little boy. He woke slowly, foggy-headed, from a deep, dreamless sleep. "My boy," she said, "my boy", and everything, everything, was OK. He went back to school that Sunday. Lance and he continued to smoke bongs together on occasion. Nothing changed, as if nothing had happened.

George stuffed the remains of the weed in his little brown pipe. He inhaled deeply, luxuriating in the fragrant perfume as he exhaled. He stretched out on the bench, as much as he could, his knees bent and his arms behind his head. The sky was dark, but he saw no stars. Who would make things OK now? My boy, my boy, thought George. He could say that to his son. My boy, my boy. He could rub two fingers on his son's back. But it wouldn't be the same. No, it wouldn't be the same, but it might be all he could do.

THE SECOND SON

The birth was similar to her first birth, but, of course, there were differences.

It was a Thursday and Edie had Bertie with her when she went for her check-up. She was a week from her due date. She always had Bertie with her. He was three, and he was her everything. Her midwife was on the Upper West Side of Manhattan; Edie was still at the same hospital, even though it was far from her house in Carroll Gardens, Brooklyn.

"You're going to go into labor soon. Why don't we strip your membranes now," said Jenny, her midwife, "that way your husband can come and get Bertie, take him to wherever he's going for the night. That way it's all under control."

Edie felt a physical pulling in. "No. No. I don't want to do that." They had stripped her membranes when she was giving birth to Bertie, when she'd been deep into labor. It had hurt like hell. "I don't want to force it." The midwife shrugged, but she was annoyed.

On the long subway ride home—Bertie loved the train, he was in heaven—Edie's breath came shallow and fast. She was afraid. She had hoped the second time around she wouldn't be so afraid, but she'd been just as afraid the whole damn pregnancy as she'd been the first time.

It took almost an hour to get home. Her feet hurt, even though she'd been sitting the whole time on the train. Bertie fell asleep, so she had to carry him home. It was less than two blocks, but still. She was very pregnant, and he was nearly three. And as she walked up the few steps to their new home, she felt a sharp pain in her abdomen. She had to put Bertie down to get her keys and he cried. Inside, she tried to put him back to sleep on the couch, but it was too late. He was awake, tired and grumpy. She felt another sharp pain and her hands began to shake. She was in labor. The midwife had been right. She'd been foolish.

Their plan was to call John Weeks, their one true friend, a graying, hard-drinking man who had dinner at their house once a week or so. She called him first, then she called Richard, her husband. John was on his way over; Bertie loved John; he was the uncle Bertie didn't have. Richard would meet her at the hospital.

"Are you ready to go?" Richard asked.

She did have a little bag packed with a toothbrush and some clean underwear. "It could take awhile to get there. And second births can go faster than first ones. I better get going." Bertie had only taken ten hours. And she'd labored at home for a lot of that. She'd only been at the hospital for four of those hours before he made his entrance.

The minute John arrived she called a car service. "Thanks, John."

"No problem. Bertie and I will be fine. Won't we, buddy?"

Bertie crawled up on to his lap and started to take off his glasses.

"I love you, Bertie. I'll be home soon. With your new baby brother." She grabbed him off of John's lap and kissed him. He squirmed. "I love you, too, Mommy."

The car honked. She waddled out to it. It was a clean, warm March day. Gone was the darkness and dirty snow of winter and the hot, filthy summer had not yet arrived. It was the perfect day to have a baby, Edie tried telling herself.

The labor pains seemed to be coming quickly. There was traffic on the bridge. She lay down in the back of the car. She noticed the driver look into his rearview mirror and give her an unkind stare. For some reason, this really bothered Edie and she began to breathe too quickly. The driver of the car Richard and she had taken when Bertie was born had been jolly, congratulatory.

She tipped the driver well, even if he'd been unfriendly. Richard was there. The midwife, Jenny, was not, but would be shortly. She felt happy to have the same midwife. She liked Jenny. The nurse began doing various things, taking her blood pressure, her temperature.

"You have a temperature." She said nervously.

Jenny walked in then.

"She has a temperature." The nurse said to Jenny.

"How high?" Jenny took the thermometer away from her. "It's not that high. You're fine."

Edie's heart was racing now. Fear, fear, fear. How could everything be fine if she was about to split apart, to cleave in two?

The contractions came harder. She walked around the room. It was a big room—a "birthing" room, and this was nice. Richard sat in a chair, looking miserable and useless. Jenny sat in another chair, reading *Newsweek* and occasionally smiling and offering some support.

Edie walked to the large window. They were on the eleventh floor. Below was Tenth Avenue. Cars and people went about their business, while she was up here, about to have a baby. It seemed strange, that the whole world wouldn't stop. Another baby. Another boy. Another Bertie, that was what she wanted. When Bertie turned two and she was so in love, she decided to try and get pregnant again; she wanted another one.

And the time had come. Looking out, she saw the deli where Richard had bought her a sandwich earlier. She had eaten it hungrily, but now she wondered if that had been a mistake. Water trickled down her leg. Just like that. There had been no need to break her water, no. But now the contractions would really begin. And then what? Oh, no, the pain. Oh, no, who would this child be? She turned to Richard.

"Please go. Please go outside."

Jenny looked up, grumpily. It wasn't nice to ask your husband to leave the delivery room. But

Edie had done it when Bertie was born, too. Yes, she didn't want him there. He was no help. A contraction drove her to her knees.

"Leave."

On her knees now, she put her hands down on the cold floor and crawled to the bed. The pain was making her hallucinate. The room undulated and swirled. Her midwife was a hazy annoyance in the room, asking something of her. What? Push? Soon, she would split in two. Who was this child? Who was he?

Looking back, there had been some signs. When she was seven months pregnant, her mother took her and Bertie to Nassau, in the Bahamas, for a week. They stayed at a lovely small hotel on the Caribbean Sea, a hotel made up of fifteen bungalows that sat up on stilts. The beach in front of the bungalows was small but calm and warm. She was there without Richard for the first five days; he was moving them into their new home and she wouldn't be any help unpacking. It was nice of him, she knew, to do the work while she sat on the beach. And yet, she resented being grateful, as if carrying their child in her womb was nothing for which to be grateful.

Bertie was so happy to see his Nana. Edie was unabashedly grateful for her mother right now. It was a wonderful feeling, this gratitude, as Edie had spent most of her adolescence resenting the woman. Edie and Bertie's bungalow was at the end of the beach, away from the restaurant and the entrance, which was guarded by a black man in uniform. It was painted a bright green and the room was round, with a large bed sitting high in the middle. She could hear the ocean, feel the wet sea air. At night, she'd pull a thin blanket over the two of them and listen and feel. The ocean and the movement inside of her that always started at night. The baby inside her sloshing and flipping around, occasionally a spot of her stomach would jump out as a foot or hand pushed. Next to her, her son slept and made gentle breathing noises. She leant into him and smelled his skin; the smell of a baby still. He was not yet three. It was hard for her to sleep.

"Let's go to the botanical garden," Edie suggested to her mother.

They drove their rented car to the center of the island, where a small white house stood, surrounded by blooming bushes. Inside, an elderly English woman sat behind a desk. They paid a small entrance fee, and then walked out the back of the house onto a dirt path. It was not a big botanical garden by any means. The day was unusually hot and humid, or it felt that way to Edie; perhaps it was because they were away from the cool breezes of the sea. Edie's mother seemed irritated by the heat, as was Edie herself. She wanted to walk around quickly, and then get back to her room.

Bertie ran off in front of them. Edie's mother held her mouth in that way that showed her annoyance.

Mom, can you chase him? Please? I don't want him touching anything he shouldn't."

Without saying anything to her daughter, her mother went after Bertie.

Most of the path was shaded. But the air was so thick. Edie could no longer see her mother or son, but she could hear them. A small wooden bench came into view and Edie made for it and sat. She spread her legs wide; her crotch was throbbing with the pressure of her insides. She rested her eyes for a moment.

"Here you are!" Her mother exclaimed. "We thought we'd lost you."

"No, I just sat for a moment. The heat is fierce here."

"Mommy, mommy!" Bertie crawled onto her and his knee went into her belly.

"Careful!" She said, her voice cross. Reflexively, she pushed him off.

Her mother picked up Bertie.

"Let's go."

"Yes, let's go."

It was the last night before Richard arrived. They ate at the hotel, where the food was lovely. Edie had a glass of wine. The waiter gave her belly a look, but Edie didn't care. One glass of wine wasn't going to hurt. In bed, Bertie lay curled up next to her. He was wearing a T-shirt and a

Paula Bomer

diaper, the blanket kicked off. He moved around,
readjusted. He was sleeping lightly. The ocean's
breeze blew the batik curtains gently. The room,
even in the dark, all wood and colorful batik, was
beautiful. Edie couldn't fall asleep. She got up and
went to the bathroom. She had to go to the
bathroom all the time now. Below her room was
the open air kitchen. She decided to go down and
get a bottle of water out of the refrigerator.

As she walked out of her bungalow, a strong
sea breeze slammed the door shut behind her.
She didn't have her key. The noise had woken
Bertie, and she heard him cry out.

Her heart began to race. "Bertie! Bertie!" She
didn't know what to do. She tugged at the door.
He was too little to open it himself. He began to
cry in earnest now. She had to get back in there.

She ran to her mother's bungalow and
knocked on the door, loudly. "Mom! Mom! Help.
I'm locked out and Bertie's alone! Help!"

Her mother came to the door, half asleep, a
robe wrapped around her. "What?"

"The door slammed and I don't have my key
and Bertie is alone..."

"OK, OK. Calm down." Her mother led her
down the dirt path. The wind was strong, the air
cool. "We'll go find someone who can open the
door."

"But Bertie's awake now. I'm going back there.
Can you come with someone? Find a key?"

"Fine. Go. I'll be there."

Edie ran back to her bungalow, the wind and sea loud in her ears. It wasn't until she was at the steps of her room that she could hear Bertie wailing. She crouched at the door, her belly pushing up on her chest. "I'm here, Bertie, Mommy's right here. I'm coming in soon."

He was alone in a dark, strange room and she'd left him there. She looked out at the sea, Bertie's voice in her ears, crying out for her.

Like the eye of a storm, Edie had a moment of complete clarity. "OK," she said to Jenny. "I'm going to push him out." In a gush of salty blood, a large, red-haired baby boy came out. She was free now. Jenny passed him to her and he cried loudly and wetly squirmed around. She tried holding him to her breast, but he flailed and screamed.

"He's a loud one," Jenny said, smiling.

"Is he OK?" She wanted to count fingers, but she didn't. He seemed OK. But she was still scared, scared something was wrong. It was all so different. When they had passed her Bertie, it had been a moment of comfort. The minute Jennie held Bertie up to her, she knew he was perfect. She looked at her son, her new son, her second son. She thought he was ugly. Richard came to her then and put an arm on her. He was shaking, his hand was trembling. Jenny had let him back in.

"You did it, honey. You did it. Look." Were there tears in his eyes? No. But he looked spent and relieved.

"Yes. Let's call him Charles. Let's call him Charlie."

Richard smiled. "Good. Let's."

Jenny examined them both. Everything was fine and they were free to go home.

"He's bigger than Bertie was. And louder," Edie said.

"The comparisons start already," Jenny said. "You might want to just take him for who he is."

Edie bristled. She was just speaking her thoughts.

They returned home together that afternoon. John Weeks was sitting in the rocking armchair that Edie had used to rock and nurse Bertie. Next to it was a brand new footstool. "A present for the Mommy," John said as they came in and Edie spotted the footstool. He stood up to give her the chair.

"Where's Bertie?"

John smiled.

"Bertie?" Edie called out, anxiety in her voice. "Bertie where are you?"

Bertie leapt out from behind the couch. Her boy. She was holding Charles.

"Look Bertie, you have a baby brother." Suddenly, she could see this meant nothing to him. He wasn't yet three, he didn't know what a baby brother was. He barely knew his colors and numbers.

Later that night, after they had ordered take-out—something Richard hated, but Edie was too tired to cook—and drank beer with John Weeks, Richard went down to the office to check his email. He couldn't stand missing one day of work. Edie was sitting in her chair with her feet on the new footstool. Charlie cried his loud, alarming cry and Bertie looked up from where he was playing with blocks in front of her. He was wearing red striped pajamas—Edie's favorite.

"He's noisy!" Bertie said.

"He just cries when he's hungry," Edie lied. It came back to her in flashes—the crying Bertie, crying when he was hungry, when he was tired, whenever. She'd thought he had colic. But no. "What else is a baby to do?" said her pediatrician. "They can't speak yet. They only know how to cry."

Edie held the strange-looking creature against her breast and she felt the slight burn of his hungry mouth. Her breast swelled and the milk came. She closed her eyes. It was like a drug, the letdown of the milk, the hormones shooting through her blood. When he was done, she put Charlie in the new crib upstairs. Bertie had followed her halfway up the stairs.

"I'm coming right back down," she said.

He looked suspicious.

"Come." she said, and she picked up her boy, the boy she always carried, even in those late stages of pregnancy when it was very hard. And yet he was heavier to her now, strangely, even though she wasn't pregnant anymore. Carrying him to the chair where she had just nursed

Charlie, she felt a rush of blood between her legs. It had been less than twenty-four hours since she'd given birth. She sat heavily. Bertie squirmed into her body, curling his legs into her lap. She took his hand in hers, his three-year-old hand. She noticed his dirty fingernails and she put his hand up to her face and smelled it. It smelled unclean—they had skipped a bath tonight—like a boy's hand, a hand that played and ate and was in the world, the big, dirty world.

"Your hand is so big, Bertie. I never...I never noticed."

Bertie looked at his hand as if seeing it, too, for the first time.

She closed her eyes, leaned her head against the chair. Gone, gone. He wasn't her baby anymore. "Come," she said. "Let me read you a book. Time to go to bed, OK?" She set him down.

"Carry me," he said, and he thrust his hands up to her, to be picked up.

The inside of her legs throbbed as she stood up. "I can't Bertie. Not just now. I'm sorry. I can't."

April came and Charlie grew fat. He nursed every few hours at night and Edie was exhausted, as exhausted as she'd been with Bertie. One morning, after a particularly brutal night of much nursing and diaper changings, she made the mistake of catching her reflection in the bathroom mirror. Her face was sallow and blotchy. She looked awful. She felt awful. Bertie came bounding in, full of life.

"Mommy, play trains with me."

"Just a minute Bertie, I need to get some coffee first. I'm very tired."

After a cup of coffee, she helped Bertie set up a train track in the living room. Charlie began to cry in his crib. She went up to get him, a red-faced squalling little football. No, he was already bigger than that, more like a watermelon. He continued to holler as she brought him downstairs.

"Mommy, make him stop!" Bertie covered his ears.

"She sat down and lifting her shirt, put him on her breast. It took a minute, but then he settled.

"Play trains, mommy!" He was sitting on his knees, holding a blue train, looking at her imploringly. Her breast swelled and she felt the milk come sharply. "I'll be Gordon, you be Deisel."

"I can't right now. I'm feeding Charlie."

Charlie began to cry again. Edie tried switching breasts. He kept crying. Bertie didn't play with his trains; he watched them as they struggled.

"Make him stop."

"I'm trying, Bertie, I'm trying."

"Play trains with me."

"I can't." Edie felt anger rise up in her. Charlie continued to howl. She stood now and began pacing, as she had last night at one moment, pacing, trying to get him to nurse, to settle. Her arms ached. Her face went hot.

Bertie stood, too, and followed her around as she paced in the living room. "Put him away, Mommy! Put him away!"

"I can't, Bertie."

"Why not?"

"I can't, Bertie."

His face fell. It wasn't the first time she'd seen him disappointed, but the look on his face—it killed her. She was holding Charlie so tightly now, maybe that was what was making him scream. She tried to relax.

"Go, Bertie. Go play trains. Just stop following me."

Bertie sulked away, and Edie went into the kitchen. She didn't know what to do. But that was how it was. Babies screamed, you tried all sorts of things, and sometimes, they just kept screaming anyway. Her head throbbed. She sat at the kitchen table while Charlie tried to squirm out of her hands. And what would happen if she let him? He would fall to the ground, that's what would happen. She opened the door in the kitchen that led to the small porch they had and went outside. The sun burned her eyes as if she had a huge hangover. It was nearing the end of April and already the ugly summer heat could be felt. She went back into the kitchen and noticed that Charlie was quieting. She tried to sneak around to the stairs, but there was Bertie.

"Shh..." she said.

"Put him down!" Bertie said, and Edie ran away from him, up the stairs to Charlie's room, afraid he'd wake his brother.

Later that night, when Richard came home, and Bertie had been read to, and sung to, and put to bed, and Charlie was asleep in his crib, Edie fell into her nursing chair. She was having a second glass of wine tonight. The day had been a day of survival. She felt demoralized, exhausted, slightly crazy, and full of self-loathing.

She began crying.

Richard was doing the dishes and when he came into the living room with his wine he asked, "What's wrong?"

It was his tone. He was annoyed. He hated it when she showed any weakness.

"I'm... I'm suffering."

Was it disgust? Or just anger in his face?

"I miss him. I miss my time with Bertie. I feel...I feel like I'm betraying him. Like I'm cheating on him with Charlie. And, and...I resent him, I resent Charlie. For causing this..."

"Well, *don't* feel that way." He stood up. "Jesus."

As she watched Richard go back into the kitchen and pour himself another drink, she thought, who was this man she called her husband? Had there really been a time when she made love to him, when she opened herself up to him, showed her face in the agony of pleasure to him? He was the father of her children, but that seemed almost coincidental at this moment. He was nothing to her. He was a man with a job. He was a paycheck.

"I want him back! I want my Bertie back!" She said, quietly, to herself. What was she to do? What was she to do? She stretched her mouth open as wide as it would go, throwing her head back, her eyes closed, but nothing came out of her. Then, then it started to come out and she shoved her fist in her mouth and bit down as hard as she could, so hard she tasted the salt of her own blood, muffling the animal howl from deep within her.

The next day she took Bertie to the playground. It was as hot as summer and only April; it felt like the day was mocking her. She trudged along, pushing Bertie in his stroller with Charlie strapped to her chest in a baby holder.

Bertie was happy to be in the playground; he immediately ran away from her and onto the jungle gym. A pregnant woman was sitting on the bench next to her with a double stroller in front of her. In one seat was a toddler, in the other, a baby not much older than Charlie. On the bench next to her, a four-year-old boy sat eating a cracker. Then an older girl pushed a scooter up to the woman and asked for crackers, too.

Edie stared. The woman and her daughter on the scooter were arguing.

"He got more than me," the girl said.

"Here, here's another one." The mother said, but her expression wasn't placating. Neither was her daughter's.

Edie unstrapped Charlie; her chest was damp with sweat where he had been and he, too, was wet and sticky. His hair caught the sun; it almost looked unreal, it was such a glorious shade, a deep orange.

"What amazing hair!" The woman said.

"Thanks." Edie said. It *was* amazing. She put him in the stroller in front of her. He was starting to smile and occasionally he broke into all sorts of baby cooing and laughter. He was a happy baby and it bewildered Edie. How could he be so happy when she wasn't? But his happiness was infectious, too. She leaned forward and cooed at him. Then Edie asked, "Are they all yours?" gesturing to the brood surrounding the woman. She wasn't much older than Edie, or so it seemed.

"Yes," the woman answered. "But I think I might stop now. Five is plenty. I don't know. I'd have more, too. I don't know."

"I just had my second and I'm so overwhelmed. I can't imagine..."

"Just wait. Soon enough, you'll want another."

"I don't know." She wanted to confide in her, but how to go about that? She thought of calling John Weeks. She needed someone, something. John would distract her and play with Bertie. Yes, she would call him later that day and invite him over for beers.

"Each time I have a baby," the woman said, leaning toward Edie now, "I keep trying to get that feeling back, that feeling you have with your first. And you never quite get it again."

Edie looked at her, stunned. The woman was a good thirty pounds overweight, her face was greasy-looking and gray hair stood out at the roots of her hair. She had "let herself go", as they once said.

She smiled. "But you can't bring it back, the past. You can only look toward the future."

Edie looked out to where Bertie was playing. He was running with two other boys around his age; they all hollered as they went.

The woman watched her watch her son. Then she said, quietly, "Have you heard the saying? Children are like pancakes, you should throw the first one out?"

Suddenly, a long, loud wail grabbed their attention. Edie stood up. It wasn't Bertie, but it was a little boy standing next to him. She went to them.

"What happened?"

"That boy hit me," cried the other boy and he pointed to Bertie.

"Bertie? Did you hit him?"

Bertie made a face and clenched his fists.

"Say you're sorry, Bertie."

"No."

"Say you're sorry!"

"I'm sorry," Bertie said, and then he began to cry.

Edie was stunned. She grabbed him by the arm and yanked him back to the stroller. She strapped Charlie back on and pushed Bertie down into the stroller and started off. She looked back at the woman who'd been sitting next to her. She was smiling, but it wasn't friendly. It was something else. Something like satisfaction.

When they got home, Bertie was still sniffling. Charlie was asleep and she put him in his crib and then ran back down to Bertie.

"You're bad!" she yelled. Anger coursed through her.

"I'm not bad."

She grabbed his arm, roughly. "Shame on you."

"Stop it, Mommy!"

"You hit someone! You *hit* someone!"

Bertie began crying more earnestly. He tried to pull away from her, but her grip tightened.

"You're hurting my arm!"

"Dammit! Dammit!" She was screaming now. She let go of his arm abruptly. He had been pulling away from her, so when she let go, he fell hard. Crying, he looked up at her; it was the first time she saw fear in his eyes.

Edie started to cry. She sat in her chair and wept with her head in her hands.

"Mommy, mommy! Don't cry. I'm sorry, I'm sorry."

"No, Bertie, it's not you. No, no. I'm just sad."

"Don't be sad, Mommy, don't be sad."

He walked up to her and put his little hand on her cheek. He was comforting her and it was all wrong. *He* was her baby, she was supposed to comfort him. No, no, it was all wrong.

"Come, come sit on my lap."

He crawled up on her, with all of his smells of the playground and sticky juice and cracker crumbs.

"I'm sorry I hit that boy."

"I know you're sorry. Just don't do it again. It's OK. It's OK." She said, stroking his hair, but she was lying. What had she done by letting herself really feel things, love, loss, pain? Wouldn't it have been better to not have felt anything at all? She'd had a boyfriend in AA years ago who'd said, feelings can't kill you. It was part of the AA philosophy and had something to do with him not drinking anymore, with letting himself feel and not try to numb himself with alcohol. But she'd answered, "Of course feelings can kill you. They are the only thing that can kill you." He broke up with her shortly after that conversation. But she'd meant it, she knew it then, but not like she knew things now. No, not like now.

"I love you, Bertie." She said. She stroked his soft curls, his sweet, three-year-old head. He was still here, he was. But he was leaving her and she didn't want him to. He wasn't her everything anymore, too, and that was no fault of his. No she wanted him to be her baby forever, forever. She wanted him, and no one else, she wanted him all

over again. Then Charlie started to cry and she
pushed Bertie off her lap to go get him.

A GALLOPING INFECTION

After they carried his wife's body out of the two bedroom house they'd been renting all week at The Golf Club of Key West, after the police had left, James Ordway thought many things, quickly, all in a row, and imagined them as a list on a piece of paper.

He no longer would have to disappoint her. He, who'd never committed adultery in the eight years of his marriage, could fuck new women. He no longer had to glimpse her aging, sagging, naked body in the bright morning light. He no longer had to worry about how her bitter, tired and nasty behavior would affect their two sons. He no longer had to listen to her speak insecurely and incorrectly and childishly in front of people who made her nervous, in other words, just about everyone she didn't know very well (her trailer park childhood in Illinois had never fully left her). He wouldn't have to look at the dark roots growing in on the top of her head, her brassy dyed hair rough and desperate-looking. He could get rid of her two annoying cats, whose litter box disgusted him, and to whom he was allergic. He never again had to deal with her truly hateful and grasping sisters. And although he deeply appreciated her dinners at night, he'd never have to eat them again, which filled him with relief. Why? If he appreciated them, why did he also feel relief at not eating her regular meals? His mind wandered from the list...how relief and appreciation? That strange force of nature, ambivalence.

He supposed he was trying to cheer himself up. He was, and always had been, an optimist. Or, as Kelly had put it, in denial.

Somewhere she'd read that people who suffered depression were too realistic. They saw things too clearly. This was not James's problem. But it had been hers. She tried taking Paxil for awhile, but remarked she preferred reality, depressing or not. "And anyway," she told him, when she announced she was over taking Paxil, "I'm only unhappy because our marriage sucks. Nothing is wrong with me. I don't have a chemical problem. You're just a shitty husband."

Now, that was true, and James had always known it to be true, but he comforted himself with the fact that he wasn't the shittiest husband out there. No, that award would go to one of the husbands of Kelly's "friends", or acquaintances rather, the women she dealt with in her daily life of taking the boys to school and lessons and the playground. Perhaps Carl, her friend Gigi's husband would be the poster boy for the world's shittiest husband. Carl traveled two weeks out of the month, and when he was home, he went out every night. Gigi had confessed to Kelly she thought her husband might be having an affair. Drunkenly, one night during a ladies night out, Gigi said to Kelly that Carl and she hadn't had sex in three years.

"And so I said, what are you going to do about it?" Kelly related to James that night, smoking a cigarette on their back porch in Brooklyn. "I mean, no marriage is perfect. But three years? And she acts like it's no big deal. I said, aren't you going to see a therapist? She laughed at me. Really. Like trying to fix your marriage was some kind of joke. She doesn't feel any responsibility to even try to make it a better marriage." James had been watching ESPN when she arrived home that night, drunk and wanting to gossip. Kelly had dragged him away from a great basketball game to tell him about Gigi and Carl. At the time he thought, Hypocrite. As if your marriage were so perfect.

But then there came a point, a few years ago, when their marriage seemed kind of perfect, if not only or especially in comparison to everyone else they knew. The miseries people had! No sex, no money, women still married to their own mothers, not their husbands. Six hours of TV a day. Women eating two entire Entenmann's cakes in one sitting in front of Kelly, as if this were normal. Women hating their sons and loving their daughters. Eventually, Kelly stopped trying to make friends, and James couldn't really blame her. But he did anyway. He wasn't convinced that feeling better than others was the best they could do. Of course, he did nothing about it. And they had problems as well, but nothing dramatic. Kelly drank and smoked. This was their biggest problem, according to James. She rarely behaved out of control. But she'd get woozy and quiet, or worse, talkative and boring at night. James was their biggest problem, according to Kelly. His coldness. The way he just ignored his wife and kids when he didn't like what they had to say. The times where he didn't seem connected to the family at all, just like some floating big man in the house, who co-habited with the rest of them. This, according to Kelly, is what exhausted her, made her bitter and bitchy. When confronted by her, James just ignored her.

"See? See?" she said, as he stared into a magazine or walked slowly into another room. "And you wonder why I drink? You're not here. Hello! You don't even care."

Anyway, now she was dead. Now, their two boys sat watching cartoons. Will's stern face was swollen and blotchy, but he was pretty focused on the screen. Jamie, their three-year-old, didn't quite get what had happened, but it would sink in as the days went by. James walked into the narrow room, toward his sons. They'd never rented here before. Kelly had found the house online and was more or less happy with it. That was a relief for James. The last thing he wanted was her ruining another vacation by bitching the whole time about what exactly wasn't perfect about their plans. Fucking control freak.

James stood there for a moment, watching his boys watch TV. Then he went back to the front of the house, thinking he'd sit out on the front steps. He sat down and the Florida sun shone hotly on him. Two gray-haired, pink-and yellow-shirted golfers walked by and stared at him. Had they seen the ambulance? The police car? Probably. Maybe he should go inside and hide. Shamefully. Or respectfully. Maybe he should keep making phone calls. Turning his face toward the sun, he decided not to do anything for a moment. He decided to stay right there. It was a strange development, the Golf Club. Everyone hid in their cars or in their little, uniform houses. The quiet was eerie, really, not comforting. It was not the quiet of, say, the country. It was the quiet of a highly developed area where many of the houses were empty most of the time, being second homes, and the people who were there kept to themselves. As if hiding something.

Everyone has something to hide, thought James.

She was sick before they left. Every winter, she got a terrible sinus infection. This time, she also had a bronchial infection. He came home from work the day before they left for Florida and she was lying on the couch, a box of tissues in her lap and a pile of dirty tissues next to her. "I'm sick. Really sick. They X-rayed my lungs and I don't have pneumonia but I have a bronchial infection and a sinus infection, like always. The doctor said I can't smoke. That my lungs are a mess. I'm scared."

And here was the thing. Every year she got sick and she got scared, and she cut back on the cigarettes and booze for awhile, but as soon as she started to feel better, she went back to her old ways. A bottle of wine at night, followed by five or ten or more cigarettes. It was one thing when they first met ten years ago. Then, for whatever reason, James found it sexy. European or something. For a while now, since the kids arrived actually, he'd found it disgusting. On the plane, she ordered a glass of wine.

"I thought you were on antibiotics? You're not supposed to drink while taking antibiotics," he said to her.

"I'm not taking the antibiotics," she said. "It would ruin my vacation."

Indeed. From the first night of their arrival. She coughed and gagged up stuff, spitting it into tissues. Then she'd look into the tissue. God, to have to see her peering into her foul tissues! Like looking into her own asshole. The rage was so intense that he'd...walk away. Nasty, nasty woman. He noticed bottles of Advil and aspirin and all sorts of pain relievers and decongestants and cough medicine around the rental house. After a day at the beach and in town walking around—they'd had beautiful weather, divinely sunny and moist and warm but not hot, not stifling—she'd asked him to stop by Walgreen's. "My head is still killing me," she'd said, and returned with a white paper bag of more drugs and new boxes of tissue.

At night, after the kids were asleep, her eyes were glassier than usual. Now, Kelly's eyes were often a bit glassy. That happens to people who drink a bottle of wine a day. And she was flushed, but again, people who drink red wine were often flushed at night. And of course, they had spent a good part of the day in the sun, which gave them all a flush. And so. And so James thought, how was he to know?

But he did kind of know. Slowly knowing something. The idea occurred to him. The idea that Kelly was really sick, that something was really wrong.

The night before she died, he emptied the garbage pail in the upstairs bedroom where they slept. He carried it downstairs, annoyed and disgusted—why didn't she bring her snot-rags down to the kitchen garbage herself? Pig, he thought. The kitchen lights were on brightly and Kelly lay in the living room alcove, visible to him, coughing and lying there in front of the television, a blanket over her despite the heat—and as he dumped the tissues into the garbage, he looked down at what he dumped out.

Why? Why does one look at a loved one's snot and filth? Just normal curiosity? The desire to hate? The desire to know?

The dirty tissues, dripping black and red, sent up a strong, acrid scent as they tumbled into the kitchen garbage. Blood and...blood and what? James looked away. What else was he to do? He looked away with disgust. Sloughing the foulness off with a quick shake of the head.

He had not always been disgusted by Kelly and he wasn't sure when it started, but he had been disgusted by her, with her, on and off now, for some time, because they lived together, because they were growing older together.

The night before she died, they lay sleeping next to each other, not closely though, because of the king size bed. They had watched a mundane drama next to each other on the couch earlier. It ran late, and they were tired. When they went up to bed, James fell asleep immediately. Hours later, in the quiet dark of the middle of night, she woke him. Wheezing, gasping, her eyes bulging with fear. "Something's wrong, James. Something's wrong..."

"What? What...?" He was barely awake.

"I can't breathe. My heart." She started coughing so loudly. He shushed her automatically. "Shhhh, don't wake the kids." He was so tired. He just wanted to sleep.

Then she put a hand on his shoulder, a hot, fierce hand. "You don't know what they want from me. You can't see them. You don't see anything. You don't see." Is that what she said? How could he really remember, after all that had happened since then? He carefully removed her pinching fingers from his shoulder and fell asleep.

The next morning, she appeared fine. Making coffee and then sitting on the couch with the kids in front of the cartoons.

"Hey, do you want to go see a doctor here?"

"No." she answered right away, without looking up from the cartoons.

He went and sat next to her. She looked awful underneath her browned skin. No suntan could hide the truth of her inner life, her sickness. Her face was a mass of hanging flesh. Her hair seemed to barely cover her scalp. He smelled toothpaste and suntan lotion and something else. The something else was not a good smell and it pushed him up and away from her and back into the kitchen to get a coffee.

He had, at one point, truly loved this woman. People do change. It is not true that people don't change. The only thing is that they almost always change for the worse. Occasionally some miserable ugly person blossoms into a happier self later in life. But Kelly had not been miserable or ugly. And perhaps she had only one way to go. It's that she went that way so quickly, so effortlessly, that James barely noticed it happening. Before he could do anything, before it registered with him, Kelly had turned into a lonely, bored outcast who had no pleasure in life. Her face and body lost all joy, all hope, all generosity. Her dead spirit took over her very body.

Once, when they were in their early twenties and newly engaged, they had drinks at the Plaza Hotel in Manhattan. Afterward, they took a carriage ride around Central Park. Their drinks had been insanely expensive, the ride seemed silly and not worth it, and yet, and yet. And yet Kelly glowed with appreciation, with gratitude.

Her head slightly bowed, her eyes wet with life and wonder. She was humble and small and happy to be alive, giving off warmth that James soaked up as he wrapped his arm around her while they walked back to their apartment. He used to soak her up. Just being next to her, just letting his body be next to her body, this was where he got his strength in the past.

And now where was he to go for strength? It had been years since he sought it from her. There had been his work and his children. And he had let himself not be strong; he had let himself be exhausted.

The night she died, he'd seen her come back from the bathroom. Half asleep, deep in the night, he saw her. She wore a thin white nightgown and her arms were glowing red, slick with damp. She coughed so loudly that he sat up, the noise had startled him so. Her naked hands were held over her mouth and as she pulled them away from her shaking face, a dark wetness dripped from her fingers to the ground. "I'm dying. I think I'm dying and I'm scared", she said.

"We'll go to the doctor in the morning," James said quietly, "you'll be fine." Had he believed that? But no, James believed in nothing anymore. He just knew what to say when something was supposed to be said.

"I'm so scared," she said, rubbing her filthy hands up and down on her gown. Her voice was not her own anymore. James reasoned, there in the middle of the night, that she wasn't making sense because he didn't recognize her voice.

"Go to sleep. Just go to sleep."

As she approached the bed, a smell so poisonous came upon him that he quickly hid his face in his pillow and curled himself on the very edge of his side of the enormous mattress. There, like that, as far away from death as he could get himself without actually leaving his wife alone in the room, he slept next to her, as whatever was left inside of her stopped existing altogether. He did not feel shame in thinking about this. But he did feel wonder. How can we live so? Die so? It barely seemed possible that their lives could be so cheap. Could it be his wife died because she didn't live? Oh God, why didn't he do something? Why did he just let her be so sick? Why did she let herself get that way?

They were not brave people, not in the face of life, and now, clearly, not in the face of death. Soon, the chill of her death would come over him, he felt it in the distance of his own body. The sun in Florida could only do so much to warm him. He would miss her in the way he would miss an arm that's been cut off. He'd be ashamed, as if something were physically wrong with him and this wrongness were obvious to the world. This would be his way to sorrow, through shame and humiliation, through the public recognition of his broken life.

The phone rang and it startled James. And, with the phone ringing (he would not answer it), he turned his head away from the street, into the house and saw his two children coming toward him, through the darkened narrow passage that was their rented home, their faces shadowed and hidden, featureless creatures, running toward him, toward where he sat outside in the sun. Fear gripped him. Why had they stopped watching TV? Oh, God, if they just would never stop watching TV, everything would be OK! They came at him, like monsters, red and burnt and huge-seeming from where he sat. He didn't want to meet them—not now, not yet.

They were just his children. But they would want to know thing he couldn't tell them. They were coming. So fast, and soon, they would be on him like animals. Crawling all over him. He was not prepared, no he was not, and it didn't matter.

HOMESICK

When John met Louisa, it was 1963. He was twenty-four years old, a graduate student from Middlebury College studying in Paris, and recently discharged from a mental hospital where he had recuperated from a nervous breakdown. His delicate features—fine bones, narrow face, and sensitive, liquidy eyes—accented his fragility. He chose to sit next to Louisa in a French Literature course at the Sorbonne because she was the most beautiful girl in the classroom.

She was not French, as he was soon to discover, but Austrian. She had long, thin legs that she crossed and uncrossed nervously. Her beauty was her strongest asset and she used it relentlessly. Soon John discovered that she was hungry, that she worked in an exporting company as a secretary during the day, as a nanny at night and on the weekends, and rarely spent her precious salaries on food. Rather, she paid for two courses at the Sorbonne in weekly installments and just made the rent for a room in the Latin Quarter that had a shared kitchen and bath.

He bought her dinner—which she ate so ravenously it frightened him a bit—and kissed her goodnight, wetly, on the lips. Louisa was taken aback by the forwardness of his behavior, but thrilled as well. She had had a few suitors of interest. But the American was to become her husband. She didn't exactly know it at the time, but she was in Paris to marry well, to get out of her small Austrian town where laboring men like her father beat their families and women bitterly spent their lives doing housework and minding children. Upon leaving her father's house, she claimed it was purely for an education that she was on her way to Paris. Her family scoffed at her search for a better life: they would not give her a shilling.

Six months later, after nineteen-year-old Louisa had lost her virginity to John, (running in tears to confess her great sin to a priest the morning after) he was supposed to return to the States, to his hometown of Memphis, Tennessee. He said, "If only I wanted to marry you." She bit her lip and asked him to drive her to Italy where she waitressed at a resort during the summers. He obliged.

They drove to Italy in a small, black Volkswagen Bug that John had rented for his stay in Paris. Two hours passed on their trip to Italy, the sky darkened, and John realized he could not drop Louisa off and leave her forever. He asked her, in a practical manner, there in the car, whether she would marry him. She said yes. He said that she would need to be careful and not drop the babies, because Louisa was a clumsy girl and dropped everything and tripped on everything. They turned the car around to drive back to Paris, but first, John pulled over to the side of the road to make love to Louisa in the back of the tiny car. They were both, separately and secretly, very excited about the turn of events. After they pulled their clothes back on and wiped their faces with the backs of their hands, they returned to the front streets and continued the drive. It was dark now, and although they couldn't see Paris, they knew it lay somewhere before them.

His mother, Edith, flew over for the wedding that took place in a small, dreary Catholic church in Leoben, Austria. She wasn't happy with Louisa. Not for her John, her baby, her favorite son who really was quite needy, what with his condition. The girl could not speak English and was poor, not to mention Catholic. But here it was. Her son gave her no choice. And to think that Eleanor back in Memphis had her hopes set on John! Eleanor, Edith thought, would have provided a stable life for her boy. She was from a good family, had a good heart, was active in the church, and because of her lame leg (from polio) couldn't complain about John's condition. But this Louisa! Did she even know about John's mental problems? Would she leave him? Would she break his heart? Edith, understandably, was worried. The wedding ceremony was in German and Edith couldn't understand a thing. She cried, and pretended that it was because she was moved by the wedding, but really she was very sad John was marrying this woman.

Their honeymoon was a no-frills hike through the Austrian Alps, and John and Louisa were enormously happy, climbing in silence all day except for the occasional yodeling that Louisa indulged in, which made John laugh. In the evening they ate stews and potatoes and drank beer at the inns scattered along the mountain tops. They shared dark cots in rooms with other hikers where the wool blankets had the word *Füssen* stitched on one side. Louisa had planned this honeymoon and John thought it very unromantic in some way. No privacy! But the mountains made him believe in God, with their quiet and grandeur, and he loved Louisa's sweaty, exhausted body. Their first child was conceived.

Back in the states, John continued his graduate work at the University of Wisconsin on recommendation from his mentor at Middlebury, Professor Perret. He was given an adjunct position. It was supposedly the best program for French philosophy. He had never been to the Midwest before, and he liked Madison, more or less. It was different than Middlebury and the Northeast in general, not quite as impressive really, but Madison had some character. His mental health was good and although he still was a bit nervous and sensitive, Louisa's presence stabilized him. She took good care of him. They moved into a two bedroom apartment in the graduate student housing project and Louisa kept the place clean and bright, with something delicious-smelling always coming from the kitchen.

Louisa wanted to take classes as well, but John didn't think it was a good idea. Why would she need to study anymore, now that she was his wife? Was she not happy being his wife, he teased? Of course I'm happy being your wife, Louisa answered, I just want to finish my degree. I enjoy studying. She took two classes and he said nothing more. Louisa threw up often, and thought it was because she was nervous in this new country, because she hadn't figured out yet that she was pregnant. John and she spoke French at first, like they had in Paris, but slowly, as they began to make acquaintances, they began speaking some English. Louisa's Austrian accent in English was strong and harsh sounding, and John didn't like it. He hadn't noticed it when she spoke French. Sometimes he thought, how is it that I went to Paris and came back married to an Austrian? But she was still beautiful and affectionate, and she cooked wonderful meals. He was happy with her.

Louisa was not so happy. She liked her classes and she was beginning to make some friends, but there was so much she didn't like. She hated the white, doughy bread, the weak coffee, the tasteless butter that smelled rancid with salt. In general, people in the Midwest seemed as bland as the ugly architecture and the flat landscape, and no one waved their arms when speaking, or raised their voices in enthusiasm. She began suffering panic attacks. A doctor told her to carry a brown paper bag around with her and breathe into it when she felt panicky. This helped some, but she felt ridiculous. When she figured out she was pregnant, she told John and he was delighted. She hoped that the panic would go away as the pregnancy continued.

It didn't really go away. And in some ways, her anxieties worsened. Married life was not what she imagined, and although she felt passionately about her husband—the line of his nose, the mournful tone of his constant whistling, the way his eyes betrayed deep vulnerability, these things, and more, made her knees weak—she wasn't sure she liked him. She no longer carried the paper bag around, but she didn't sleep well at night. It became more difficult to do the housework because of her large, pregnant stomach. One night after dinner, she asked John to help her with the dishes. He laughed and said in French, "Sweet thing, don't I pay the bills on time? Save them until the morning if you're not feeling well." With that, he patted her gently on her stomach and went into his office to read.

Their daughter was born in the University hospital on a blistery cold Wisconsin March day. Louisa's labor, like her pregnancy, was normal and not so difficult, but the doctor had heavily drugged her without telling her, which left her disoriented and scared, and then he gave her a huge episiotomy. As he sewed her up afterwards, looking up from where he was doing his work, he said, "And this stitch is for your husband", and winked. Then, when she wanted to breastfeed, everyone seemed disgusted. The pediatrician said, "What are you, a cow?" and laughed at her.

She nursed her daughter anyway, and as her infant suckled, she was filled with acute despair, a certain heimweh. In Austria, or even in France for that matter, things would not be this way. Everyone in Europe knew breastfeeding was good and beautiful. European doctors didn't slice away at mother's vaginas for no reason. On the flat fields of the Midwest, motherhood was not as precious or sensuous as in her homeland.

John, who had so looked forward to the arrival of his child, was bewildered. Firstly, he had thought it would be a boy. It was a girl. Secondly, she was an ugly, wrinkled little thing who screeched abominably without end in the evenings. How could he finish his dissertation under such circumstances? He rehearsed asking her to go visit her family in Austria for a few months. He knew she hated them, but he felt desperate. Things were just so bad since the baby was born! Louisa smelled of sour milk and would get up all through the night to nurse the baby. This, of course, he found disruptive to his own sleep. Here he was, with a new child, and instead of being happy, he was miserable and exhausted. His mother flew up from Memphis and was pleased they named the girl after her. But she thought Louisa held her too much and complained to John that the girl would be spoiled. John agreed with his mother, but Louisa, already getting thin again, ignored their admonishments and snuck around the house with the swaddled infant, cooing and bent over her package like some wild, crippled animal.

After John's mother left, he decided to approach Louisa at night. The baby was asleep; they had eaten a wonderful goulash, sopping up the spicy sauce with a loaf of bread, and were sitting in the tiny living room drinking a glass of wine. Louisa was knitting a sweater for the baby while trying to read a novel propped up on a table beside her. John thought she looked ravishing—her hair fell against her neck and her dark eyes glowed with exhaustion. The motion of her thin fingers and the knitting needles excited him and he went to her, pushing the sweater out of her hands, and kissed her forcefully. She wasn't healed yet from the birth, but she obliged him anyway, and he was grateful for that.

Edith became a beautiful little girl. She was tow-headed and blue-eyed and lanky, reminding Louisa of her beloved older sister, Eva, who had left the family when Louisa was only eight. Edith's manners were delicate and her voice soft. Louisa loved her more than anything and was amazed that she and John had made this creature. As Edith began talking and playing with other children, Louisa felt ready to have another baby. John's dissertation was moving along and he had that bit of money he inherited when his father died. She brought it up with him and he agreed: it was time to try for another child.

John was excited at the thought of having another child, and hoped that this one would be a boy. While he had grown to love Edith, it was as if the impression she made as a screaming infant was insurmountable in some way, and he longed for a little male child for whom he could buy train sets and toy soldiers. Louisa got pregnant easily and after the initial nauseous period, was a healthy, lovely pregnant woman. She, too, hoped it would be a boy.

This time, when arriving at the hospital in labor, Louisa shrilly commanded that no drugs be given to her. Although she hadn't managed to stop the doctor from giving her another episiotomy, ("You don't want to stretch yourself out, do you?" the doctor yelled as she tried to protest the blade coming down on her), she delivered her child without being hampered by the frightening haze of Demerol. The doctor passed her another girl, a smaller baby girl than Edith had been, with an alarming head of dark hair. She was quiet and quickly became fat. Fat and content, Louisa and John joked, and never talked of their disappointment that it was another girl. Louisa named her Greta, after her own mother, who died at the end of the war from a mysterious illness, when Louisa was just five.

Edith, sweet-tempered, beautiful, well-behaved Edith, became extremely jealous of her baby sister. Despite the fact that Greta was an easy, complacent baby, Edith couldn't stand the attention taken away from her. She threw shrill tantrums and cried dramatically, recalling her infant behavior, and so Louisa passed the baby to

John and took Edith on walks or for a drive to the store. John, bewildered at first, looked at this fat baby in his arms, his second daughter, whose dark hair had abruptly fallen out and was now growing in blond like her sister's. He had rarely held Edith when she was an infant—Louisa would barely let him. But it was not hard to care for Greta—everything he did made her happy. She never screamed all evening like her sister had. She greedily took the bottle from him when he offered it to her, sucking loudly and blissfully, often falling asleep cradled in his arms. Gradually, his time with Greta began feeling quite special, like a secret love affair. He would play Beethoven's Kreutzer Sonata and dance her around the room. He believed she loved the music, believed she understood it like he did. Now, when Edith grew antsy and demanding, he'd offer to take Greta, and encourage his wife to go out with their eldest daughter. And so Greta became his, and Edith was hers.

John finished his degree. His dissertation was received with some ambivalence. He began looking for a tenure track position and the pressure felt enormous. He lost some weight. He thought for sure he could get a position at Middlebury and he wanted badly to move back to New England. Professor Perret had been so encouraging, had so recommended studying in Wisconsin. But it didn't happen. And he thought that Professor Perret would send him a letter, an explanation of some kind. But no matter how often he checked the mail, no letter came. He kept looking for positions, but he felt depressed about it. Finally, a small university in Iowa, St. Theresa's, hired him, and Louisa and he packed up their stuff into a truck and drove the children across the plains, deeper into the heartland, to his new job.

The college was renowned for its lovely campus, but the town itself was ugly. They bought a three bedroom contemporary brick house near the university. It was supposed to be an exciting moment in their lives, but neither of them felt excited. Louisa seemed overwhelmed with the task of setting up house, what with the two girls running around at her feet, and John had grown increasingly quiet and thin. He felt as if he had not lived up to his potential, that he had not gotten a job worthy of his talent. He felt like a failure. He walked to and from the campus every day down the side of a road that was busier than he would have liked. The sun burned the back of his neck a reddish brown and he stood in front of his eager students, ghostly pale except for the back of his neck, teaching a literature and a philosophy about which he no longer felt passionate. The young women in his classes loved his gentleness and vulnerability and often approached him for questions and conversation after class. They reminded him of Louisa when he had first met her—enthusiastic, energetic, loving —and this only further added to his melancholy.

Their children grew, Edith into a slightly bossy but beautiful girl, and Greta into the center of John's heart. Louisa finally settled—her English was good, her girls were more self-sufficient—and she hired a babysitter so she could take some graduate courses in psychology. She still hated the bread, so now she made her own, and she found a place that shipped her Viennese coffee. The Midwest would never suit her, but she made the best of it. It was 1972; feminism was making a big splash on TV and even slightly on the conservative campus at St. Theresa's. Louisa, despite her attachment to home-cooked meals and a clean house, felt inspired. She made new friends and joined a women's reading group. She argued politics and smoked and drank at parties. John felt her growing away, felt her confidence and joy with her new friends and ideas, and it pained him.

The new politics were lost on John; in fact, his long-nurtured love of 16th century French philosophy and classical music barely thrived. But his love for Greta grew. The fat, happy baby had blossomed into a ruby-mouthed, coy girl, with a deeply mischievous side. She worshipped her father. Often she would exclaim that Daddy and she were going to get married, wrapping herself around his legs blissfully. Louisa, while clearing the table, would ask, What about me? What will happen to me? Greta, as if stating the obvious, would say that when she grew up, Mommy would be old and wrinkly, but Daddy would still be shiny and new. And so they would get married. Everyone laughed at this point, Edith because her little sister was so silly, Louisa and John because she was so cute and so in love with her Daddy.

And so, when John walked down the too-busy road to teach his beautiful young students at St. Theresa's, it was Greta who made it possible. And when his mind became dark and distracted—why this college, why this small town, why did Professor Perret not hire me after he recommended I study at Wisconsin, why is Louisa so distant?—he would think about his second daughter and her complete devotion to him and he would keep walking, keep teaching, and even manage the walk back home. And so he got through his days and his evenings, he managed the nights out that Louisa took to go to her book group or to some political rally, but certain things he didn't manage. He didn't manage keeping an appetite. He recognized Louisa's food as delicious, but could only eat a few bites. And occasionally his head hurt so badly that he could not get out of bed. He knew it was a matter of time before Greta could no longer bear the weight of his life. She was, after all, at this point, only a five-year-old girl.

What was he to do? If he rolled around on the floor with Greta, laughing and playing and carrying on like he was having a good time, everyone would probably think, he's having a good time. And maybe for him he was. But really the entire time, he thought, If I talk in this way and touch here, push there, and swing her around, it will appear I am having a good time. It will even feel like a good time to Greta, of this he was quite sure. His daughter could not stop touching him, pulling his ears, crawling on his lap. There was no end to it for her. But John's despair won out over all of his acting, beat down all of his genuine efforts to move through his days. It was bigger than him, and even bigger than Greta, although Greta thought nothing was bigger than her.

One Saturday, in the late morning, white-lipped and thin as a stalk of wheat, he got in the station wagon and drove away, without a word to Louisa or his children, who watched as he backed down the drive.

Louisa walked out after him, down to the street. John? This was peculiar, even for John. The day passed uneventfully. Evening drew near and Louisa became nervous. John had not returned. She had her reading group tonight and he knew it—so where was he? He had never left like this, abruptly, without saying anything. She thought of calling the police and the thought embarrassed her. Greta was asking for her father and Edith was annoyed that her mother had to pay attention to her younger sister. Usually her father took care of that. After dinner and much crying at bedtime, after the children were safe in bed, Louisa phoned the police. A few hours later, two uniformed policemen brought John home, dazed and quietly talking to himself. He had been found in a field outside of town. They spotted the station wagon on Route 31 and found him lying in the grass, in a ditch, not far from where he had parked. He was hospitalized that night. The police took him there.

This, of course, would not be the last time in their marriage that John would be "sick" and away. Louisa did not know about his previous breakdown, but when she found out, she was not surprised. She took Greta and Edith to visit him. He was heavily drugged, sewing leather belts together, a crafts activity the hospital provided for its patients. Electroshock therapy started the next day and they wouldn't be able to visit him for quite some time. Louisa's eyes filled on her way home from that first visit. Was it wrong to have wanted his help with the dishes? Was it wrong to have friends and ideas? She glanced in the rearview mirror at her two beautiful daughters, one striking and exact, the other lush and dreamy. Edith seemed even more rigid than usual—she did not like change. Greta's face was clouded over —she wanted her father. But would she ever have him again? Perhaps not, definitely not, thought Louisa, as she turned the car up the drive toward their home.

Paula Bomer grew up in South Bend, Indiana. Her fiction has appeared in *Open City, The Mississippi Review, Fiction, New York Tyrant* and elsewhere. She is the co-publisher of Artistically Declined Press, and supervising editor of *Sententia*. *BABY* is her first collection.